# CELEBRITY PASTOR

## A NOVEL OF SUSPENSE

### CRESTON MAPES

## ALSO BY CRESTON MAPES

### STAND ALONE THRILLERS
*Celebrity Pastor*
*I Am In Here*
*Nobody*

### SIGNS OF LIFE SERIES
*Signs of Life*
*Let My Daughter Go*
*I Pick You*
*Charm Artist*
*Son & Shield*
*Secrets in Shadows*

### THE CRITTENDON FILES
*Fear Has a Name*
*Poison Town*
*Sky Zone*

### ROCK STAR CHRONICLES
*Dark Star: Confessions of a Rock Idol*
*Full Tilt*

# PRAISE FOR CELEBRITY PASTOR

"*Celebrity Pastor* should be required reading as a help to recognize the trap of pride and power in any kind of prominent position. Mapes's new novel was one of the most suspenseful I've ever read, and I'm still breathless. Don't miss this one!" — **Colleen Coble, *Publishers Weekly* and *USAToday* bestselling author**

"A masterful plot spun together in a thrilling tale of betrayal and faith, in true Creston Mapes style! With a plot that will keep you on the edge of your seat, this Christian thriller delivers suspense and spiritual depth in equal measure. Don't miss out on this heart-pounding story Mapes crafted with skillful ease!" — **Bestselling Christian Suspense Author, Urcelia Teixeira**

"This story takes Christian suspense to a higher level of excellence with its multiple thought-provoking themes and spiritual truths. It will resound with many readers' life experiences. This is one of Creston Mapes's best books yet, and not to be missed!" — **Early Reviewer**

"In recent years, numerous megachurch pastors have crashed and burned, which makes the narrative of *Celebrity Pastor* all too real. Creston Mapes's latest novel crackles with intensity; it's the kind of book you want to read in one sitting if possible. Not just because it's so engaging, but because it can make each of us examine our susceptibility to the riches of this world. That's why you shouldn't skip the discussion questions at the end." — **Ken Walker, Book Editor & Freelance Writer**

"This story is raw and well-told. The deeper I got into it, the more I needed to keep reading to find out how it would be resolved. In addition, the narrator of the audiobook was absolutely perfect!"
— **Bestselling Author Robin Lee Hatcher**

"Creston Mapes offers a front-row seat to a heartbreaking cautionary tale about the dark side of a ministry swept away by fame and fortune. But far beyond the moral compromises of Pastor Neil Gentry, and all the wealth and power he has accumulated, lies a vast sea of damage and disillusionment. His family, his flock, his friends, and everyone reading the headlines exposing his narcissistic behavior will be affected. How sad that Gentry's story is such a familiar one to so many of us today. NO one writes suspense as well as Creston Mapes, and I believe Celebrity Pastor is his best thriller yet." — **Early Reviewer**

"Another sleepless night, courtesy of Creston Mapes. I've seen more than a few 'celebrity' pastors come and fall. It's always money or women, or a combination of the two. This isn't really news, so I wondered how the author would weave the mundane into the thriller that keeps me reading his books. I shouldn't have worried. With his canny storytelling and his uncanny sense of timing Mapes gave me a story that kept the pages turning way beyond my bedtime. My favorite quote in the story? 'He was not sinning. He was special.' Let the reckoning begin." — **Author Sharon Srock**

"I could not put this book down! Creston brings out the vulnerabilities of those in ministry that many of us don't even think about. I highly recommend this book!" — **Early Reviewer**

"Neil Gentry started out with his heart in the right place. However, after the popularity and power that came with a growing church, he changed. He went from preaching the Word to preaching what made him look good. This story shows what can happen to men whose ambition for power and money grow bigger than their love for God. With each chapter the tension grows. Will the power and popularity continue, or will God show his power over the people and the church?" — **Early Reviewer**

*Celebrity Pastor* is a work of fiction. Names, characters, organizations, places, events, and incidents are either products of the author's imagination or are used fictitiously. Any resemblance to actual persons, living or dead, or actual events is purely coincidental.

Copyright © 2024 Creston Mapes, Inc
Published by Rooftop Press. All rights reserved.

No part of this book may be reproduced or stored in a retrieval system, or transmitted in any form or by any means, electronic, mechanical, photocopying, recording, or otherwise, without express written permission of the publisher.

Scripture quotations from: *New American Standard Bible* (NASB) 1960, 1977, 1995 by the Lockman Foundation. *The Holy Bible,* New International Version (NIV) 1973, 1984 by International Bible Society. The New King James Version®. Copyright 1982 by Thomas Nelson.

# ACKNOWLEDGMENTS

*Thanks to my dear friend Darrell Pruitt for his wisdom and insights.*

*Continued appreciation to author buddy Mark Mynheir for his expertise in police procedures.*

*Once again, my gratitude to friend Chuck Pardoe (The Closer), for listening and bouncing ideas.*

*Big shout out and thanks to my early reader team for your time, love, and insights: Patty Mapes (wink, wink), Ken Walker, Gail Mundy, Diane Moody, Lynnelle Murrell, Rachel Savage, and Ginger Aster. Special thanks to author friend Robin Patchen for her time and attention to the early manuscript.*

*Beware of the false prophets, who come to you in sheep's clothing, but inwardly are ravenous wolves.*
MATTHEW 7:15

*My brethren, let not many of you become teachers, knowing that we shall receive a stricter judgment.*
JAMES 3:1

# ONE

HORACE STONE (*THE WASHINGTON POST*): How can a megachurch pastor—a man with thousands of people looking up to him, depending on him—fall into the kind of flagrant misconduct and moral failures of which this man is being accused? How can this happen?

**Dr. Daryl Kit (Clinical Psychologist and Trauma Expert):** First of all, let me clarify for the record that these are all only allegations at this point. The worship leader came forward, followed by several other female congregants and volunteers with complaints of flirtation, inappropriate comments, and sexual advances. It is the duty of the senior pastor—and all clergy leaders—to act in the best interest of the congregants, to maintain professional boundaries, and to refrain from using those relationshipsB for personal advantage. Relational misconduct in a pastoral relationship violates the sacred trust of ministry.

Back to your question about how this happens, let's keep in mind that the American church—not in all cases, but in cases like this—is mimicking celebrity culture. And one of the main problems with that is that some of these churches develop an insular structure. Ultimately, the pastor is put on a pedestal and gets to a point where he is not interested in anyone else's ideas, experiences, opinions, or wisdom—outside his own. Why? Because he believes with every fiber of his being that his ways are the right ways, the only ways. After all, his ways are working. The church is growing exponentially. He must be doing "God's will." He sees himself as "the chosen one." If he has an idea, it must be from God. This man believes he has created the correct culture. His way is the right way and he shuts out everything else. But in reality the pastor has grown proud and uninterested in anyone else's input.

**Stone:** There is no denying that the growth of his church has been jaw-dropping.

**Dr. Kit:** Without question. He is a very charismatic leader. When you combine that kind of magnetic personality with that kind of insular culture, it can be a recipe for disaster. The perfect storm if you will. The leader of that culture—really, no matter what the size of the church—is held up, he is exalted. He has absolute power. And that feeds on itself. And that insular culture creates the perfect environment for giving the pastor way too much power. It shouldn't be that way and there are megachurches that are not that way. The bottom line is that a person in this high and visible position absolutely must remain humble and teachable and accountable. I don't care if it's a megachurch or a church of a hundred members. He must remain humble and teachable.

**Stone:** Watching his teachings and hearing him talk, he seems quite genuine. His messages are indeed powerful. He's a mature, middle-aged man. He knows the scriptures inside and out. It seems that his motives in getting into this were pure.

**Dr. Kit:** I have no doubt. I spoke with him in-depth several times early on and was very impressed with him. He had a firm grasp of the Bible and spent a great deal of time preparing his messages. He seemed genuine in his purpose. I think what happens is, yes, people like him start out well-intentioned. But . . . pride . . . pride is such a powerful thing. You have to understand, once people start looking to you for everything, coming to you for everything, you begin to think, wow, they are looking at me differently—like a star. You are in demand. Everyone wants to be around you, associated with you, noticed by you. Celebrities start coming to your church. You get invited to the White House. You're a big deal. That's quite a feeling. Without realizing it, your pride inflates and power becomes an idol. That prominence is intoxicating. You've got to have it. You've got to *keep* it. After years of people coming to you, asking for advice, seeking counsel, wanting to be near you—you can easily start thinking you are the king of the castle.

**Stone:** Okay, I get it about the power trip. But it seems a far jump to go from a power trip to the kind of misconduct within ministerial relationships that we are talking about in this case. This man is a devoted pastor. He has repeatedly expressed his love for God. He's devoted his life to the church and bringing others to God. Dozens if not hundreds of churches have spun off from his concept. He has a wonderful wife and children. How does it get so dark for him? How does he stoop so low—if, of course, the allegations are true?

**Dr. Kit:** *(Long pause and sigh)* When you have insulated yourself like this, when you are "the man," you can lose objectivity. You can lose your bearings. Reality becomes blurred. You think you're so powerful that you can get away with anything. It's a lie, really. Nobody is immune to this. At some point, the person becomes self-deceived. And the problem is, with many of these celebrity pastors, there are no safeguards in place. Why? Because the pastor on the pedestal has surrounded himself with "yes men" and "yes women." There should be an objective board in place with people who aren't his buddies, people whom he did not hand pick, people who will call him out and do the right thing. Instead, he's surrounded himself with people who can be manipulated. They are not going to hold him accountable because they are in awe of him. The board he should have would be comprised of people outside his group of friends. They would be weighing things for the good of the church. They would meet with him regularly. They would have access to his phone and computer and calendar and itinerary and budget. The pastor would be forced to listen to them. They would have the power to reprimand him, to fire him even. But, apparently, the opposite of that has been happening in this case. This man had private phones, a separate email server, and his own church credit cards. He believed he had all the answers and he was not seeking input from anyone. He would not receive input. He believed he was infallible. He believed he was too powerful to be caught.

**Stone:** What about personal accountability? I know that many people of faith have what they call accountability partners to discuss the tough topics and to walk through those things together.

**Dr. Kit:** Part of the problem is, because of the church culture, pastors often don't talk about stuff like that if they are the leaders. They are afraid if they do talk to someone about their problems or trials or temptations, they are going to get found out and get fired. But, yes, they absolutely should have someone—a friend, a confidant. The perfect person would be a best friend who's known him forever. That person sees you for who you really are, as a normal, imperfect, regular guy, not as a famous, world-renowned pastor. They know you are really nothing more than the next guy. The pastor can confide in them, "This is what is happening to me, this is where I'm going off the rails." But that doesn't happen often because they do not want to get too close to anyone.

**Stone:** I'm still having a difficult time understanding how a man of God who is on that pedestal with all those people relying on him—how he jeopardizes losing everything: his family, his reputation, his wife, his church, his career. What is the mindset there?

**Dr. Kit:** Look at King David, look at Solomon—they had affairs. This is how the pastor justifies his bad behavior when things are really spiraling out of control. The enemy comes in to destroy everything God's done. Satan fans the flames. That pastor may say to that lady in his congregation, or on his staff, "I know you have a husband, but this is special, this is going to help me and, therefore, it is going to help the church." That can be the ugly, evil, misconstrued mindset.

**Stone:** Talk about how this kind of behavior does damage to more than just the pastor and his wife and family.

**Dr. Kit:** Oh my gosh, the fallout is often widespread and catastrophic. People leave the church because of this kind of behavior; they leave God altogether, in many cases. Unfortunately, that is because they were following the man and not Jesus. Some of the worst damage is done to the people who may have been on the pastor's inner circle. When that pastor is a big celebrity like this man, and that pastor includes you in his inner circle, you can get stars in your eyes. You can get carried away with the whole pomp and circumstance surrounding this person. And, in fact, people near the top leader often receive special treatment themselves simply because they are within the inner circle; they get the crumbs from the king's table so to speak. But all the while the leader is using and manipulating those insiders. And then when that pastor falls, those around him are left devastated and often their faith implodes.

## TWO

"I don't want to be here. I'm just going to say it."

She was nervous and she was shivering because it was frigid in there.

"Pardon me, Mrs. McQue. I'm sorry. Before we get started, do you mind if I record our session on audio? It's just so I won't have to be preoccupied taking notes. My receptionist should have explained—"

"She did. I don't care. Go ahead."

Dr. Samuel Yeager set the tiny recorder on the mahogany table between them. He pressed a button and it beeped. "You were saying you don't want to be here."

"I don't, and I mean no offense to you," she said.

"Many people don't want to come to therapy at first. But many of those same people find that it becomes a great source of help and hope for them. Perhaps you'll become one of those people."

"Look, Doctor, I don't mean to be rude. Please don't take this personally, but I have a difficult time believing this is going to help me."

"Why is that?"

She chuckled, more from numbness and sheer nothingness than from anything amusing. "I don't know. It's just not the type of thing I ever imagined myself doing. Plus, I know what I'm feeling. I know what a ruin I've made of things. It's a fact that I'm the one in our marriage who messed up. Darren did nothing wrong. And, although I was pursued by this man, that doesn't matter here. None of the carnage is going away any time soon. I just don't feel there's much hope. It's just the way it is and I don't know how an outsider like you can change anything."

"Well, Mrs. McQue . . . may I call you Nicole?"

"Yes."

*Call me whatever you want, this is likely the last time you'll see me.*

"Nicole, you've been through some extremely traumatic and draining circumstances of late—things I'm certain you never imagined yourself ever having to cope with."

Her jaw tightened.

*Yeah, and most of it's my fault.*

She squeezed the armrests of the cold chair. The August sky outside was darkening. Greenery blew in the breeze just outside the office window. It was starting to rain. Finally. It'd been weeks. The plants on her tiny balcony would get watered. What a pitiful existence she had now, living in that dinky apartment. She needed groceries. She had to do laundry—at a laundromat, of all places. She thought of the girls, living with their father in the house, and that familiar sense of despair crept over her like a black cape.

Her eyes shifted back into the room. She crossed her arms and stared hard at the neatly painted, glossy white windowsill. His eyes were examining her; she could feel it. These shrinks were trained to read body language. She uncrossed her arms even though her teeth were practically chattering from the cold. What did he have the AC set on, fifty? Was that some trick they used to get people to talk—freezing them to death? Certainly, he noticed how hard she was working to just sit there without losing her marbles.

"Tell me why you're here, Nicole?" said Dr. Yeager. "What do you want out of this?"

Her head dropped to her chest and she sighed, close to tears.

He waited patiently.

"Everyone has told me I should do this." She tried to slow her breathing and not cry. "I guess I feel I owe it to my husband, my girls. Our parents. Plus, if Darren and I end up in court, if he divorces me, I want to be able to say I had counseling. I'm just being honest. I was told I should do it."

"That's fine." He looked at his notes. "You mentioned on the phone you felt like you were drifting. Let's talk more about that feeling for a moment."

She set her shoulders back, inhaled deeply through her nose, and exhaled through an O-shaped mouth. "I feel like I'm all alone, out on a raft in the middle of the ocean. That's actually what I envision. All by myself, bobbing up and down, no land in sight. It's extremely depressing."

He handed her a tissue and she wiped her nose and looked up at him with watery eyes.

"When I left that church, I left everything. Everything. It was my world. Our world. My children's world."

"How long were you there?"

"Ten years. My kids grew up in that church."

"And your children are how old—"

"Think of that . . . ten years we gave our lives to that place." Her face burned with anger. She saw stars for an instant. She wiped her eyes with the tissue.

He waited.

"My girls?" she said. "I'm sorry, they're twelve and fourteen."

Dr. Yeager jotted a note and examined the notepad in his lap. He was handsome. Hard shoulders, firm chest, dark arms, slender waist. His khakis were neatly pressed and he wore a sage polo shirt and a shiny brown belt and shoes. He had on a black runner's watch, no other jewelry. No wedding band.

"In our initial phone call, I believe you mentioned you were having some challenges at work," he said. "Would you like to tell me about that?"

"I'm not used to working outside the home. Darren always worked and I was home with the girls. That's just the way we always did it; it was good for us. So, working nine-to-five is all new to me. I miss the girls." Her shoulders lurched as she fought back the emotion. "I'm lonely. I'm sad. I'm regretful. I miss the way things used to be. And of course it's my fault. I did things that can't be taken back. I don't know if Darren will ever trust me again and I can't blame him."

"Tell me more about how it used to be."
*This is what they're trained to do, they get you to ramble.*
She shook her head with remorse. "Our home was peaceful. Happy. A beautiful house. I made everyone a nice breakfast, drove the girls to school, cleaned and shopped and did laundry and errands during the day, worked on stuff for church, then I was all theirs after school and in the evenings. I was always ready to pour into them. I loved every minute of it. Darren and I had a good system down. Now . . ." Her eyes welled up with tears. "I only see them whenever we can arrange it. It hurts so badly. And when I do see them, things aren't the same." She cried as she spoke. "I can see it in their faces, in their eyes. They're hurting. They don't look healthy, not like they used to. They don't feel the same about me. They know I did something wrong."

"What is the arrangement with the girls and their father?"

"He has them." She shrugged. "They live at the house with him. I took an apartment ten miles from them. I see them when we can do it. We're both busy. There's nothing set in stone right now about how often I see them. To be honest, sometimes I'm so depressed, I don't want to see them. I don't want to bring them down."

"Do you talk about what happened with the girls?"

Her heart sank to that dark place. She couldn't stop it. The guilt was so heavy.

She remembered his face. The famed pastor. Neil Gentry. That million-dollar smile. The special attention he gave her. That quick flash of a wink. That alluring jump of his dark eyebrows. Flirting. With her! Nicole McQue. A wife. A mother. A member of his congregation. A woman ten years younger than him.

"Nicole?" Dr. Yeager said softly.

She snapped out of it and tried to collect her thoughts.

"Sorry, what did you ask?"

"If you talk with the girls about what went wrong?"

She cleared her throat. "We do, but it's all on the surface. I generalize things. I'm not positive what Darren has told them. I'm sure he's as gracious as he can be. I say things like, 'Mom made some bad decisions; Mom can't live with you right now; we'll go back to church later; Dad and Mom need time apart; you can't see your church friends for a little while, but you'll make plenty of friends at school.' That type of thing."

"Well, that's good. You're doing what you need to do in order to keep moving forward."

Nicole nodded and looked down at her hands, which were white because they were clasped together so tightly. Her solitary diamond sparkled. She had refused to take it off even though Darren no longer wore his wedding band.

"Let's go back in time a bit to when you first started attending Vine & Branches Church. Were you a religious person at the time and what drew you to the church?"

Nicole cleared her throat, glanced out the window, and wiped the corner of her eye with a tissue. Thunder rolled in the distance. Dr. Yeager handed her another tissue and she nodded thanks and took it. She forced herself to try to relax and sighed again, deeply.

"I was not a Christian; neither was Darren. Neither of us had much church background. A couple we met in our neighborhood went to Vine & Branches. They were these really happy, vibrant people. Their marriage seemed really solid. Their kids were super nice, they were teens. Very mature. Very responsible and kind. They babysat our girls. They talked about their church a lot. Darren and I were so impressed with their family. We just didn't meet children that polite very often. We wanted our kids to turn out like that. We wanted to have a marriage like theirs. So, we discussed it and decided to try their church."

"What was it like?"

Nicole shook her head and a sobby chuckle slipped out.

"Amazing. We'd never experienced anything like it. The nursery and children's program were off the charts. The volunteers were so joyful and outgoing. Our girls loved it from day one." She sounded as if she was in a daze, a tranquil moment of fond recollection. "And we couldn't believe the church service. They had a contemporary worship band, which Darren and I loved. It was like being at a concert. Dark, theater-like setting with a big screen. There were fun skits. We liked all they were doing in the community. They'd give out turkeys at Thanksgiving, have clothing drives for underprivileged neighborhoods. We were just blown away with all of it from day one. It made us feel good to be there and to be part of that community."

"And so I take it you began attending there regularly."

Nicole's mouth sealed shut.

She closed her eyes and nodded with regret.

*If only we'd never found that church.*

"We've got a few more minutes," Dr. Yeager said. "Do you want to start telling me about how you and Darren began getting involved at Vine & Branches?"

*No. No.*

All she could think about was how she'd been lured into the inner circle, seemingly hand-picked. How shocked she'd been when Pastor Neil first flirted with her, the utter disconnect of it all. This was the senior leader of a world-renowned church, ten years older than her, coming on to her, talking about things he shouldn't, making subtle romantic comments and advances.

"Pastor Neil." The term sickened her. And within twenty-four hours she would be presenting her accusations against him to the elders of his church.

That fear made her stomach bottom out.

She glanced at her watch and stood abruptly. "I'm sorry." She shook her head but couldn't find any words. Her mind had thrown up a gauntlet; there was no going past it.

Dr. Yeager stood. "There's nothing to be sorry about, Nicole. You've had a really good first session."

She frowned, nodded vehemently, and threw her purse over her shoulder. "I just . . . this is enough. It brings back too much. Bad memories."

She headed toward the door, feeling dizzy.

"You did very well," said Dr. Yeager, following her toward the door. "We'll make more progress next time, okay?"

Nicole turned to face him before leaving.

She didn't know if she would come back.

She stood there frozen, at a loss for words, her mouth hanging open.

Dr. Yeager stared at her, waiting. He was quite a tall man. He seemed genuine. And safe.

She knew if she came back, they would eventually address

Gentry's advances, and her regrets. Her guilt. The filthy details. All the humiliation. And the hatred.

"Tell you what," he said softly. "Make an appointment with Angie on the way out, or just wait. See how you feel over the next few days. I think you're going to find that talking about it with someone anonymous helps immensely."

He took a business card from his legal pad and handed it to her.

"Just call when you're ready to continue. I'll be here. And I'm very confident we can make some very positive progress."

She glanced at him one last time.

He winked.

*Just like Neil Gentry.*

# THREE

My name is Darren McQue. I'm thirty-six. Husband of Nicole, who is thirty-four. Our daughters are Dixie and Dottie; they are fourteen and twelve, respectively. Nicole and I are not together now because of all the events I'm about to describe. I have the girls. This is an ugly and sordid tale. I don't know if this will become a magazine story, a memoir, a book, or what, but I'm sharing it in order to prevent what happened to us from happening to anyone else. And maybe to bring some kind of healing to those who have been hurt by the church. I'm also doing it in hopes it will help me heal. If it just ends up being another journal entry, that's fine with me.

It was 2014 when we first visited Vine & Branches Church in Strongsville, Georgia, a suburb of Metro Atlanta. From day one, our family was mesmerized by this growing church, its senior pastor, leaders, worship band, staff, and volunteers. It was a major league production. Our daughters were just four and two at the time, but they were very content and happy with the nursery and children's church. Nicole and I—who had no strong religious beliefs before—experienced a spiritual awakening that changed our lives. Within a few months we were baptized. The girls were baptized years later on a Sunday evening at the conclusion of a weekend camp retreat.

Nicole and I were completely fascinated by the sermons that

were presented each Sunday. The pastor, Neil Gentry, forty-four, was a charming, charismatic leader who spoke with amazing authority and insight about the Bible. For us, this was a whole new world of enlightenment. God, it seemed, became real to us. Each Sunday we felt he was speaking directly to us through the sermons and the worship and even the people. We began reading our Bibles, praying with our children, and going back to listen to past sermons by Pastor Gentry, and reading his books.

For a long time, our lives had become the best they'd ever been. We were a happy family. We had never known that kind of pure joy. Nicole and I had rekindled our love and partnership. The girls were happy and making friends. We were on a spiritual high. It was like a mountaintop experience.

So, naturally, we wanted to get involved with the church. Our goal in doing so was to promote and share what we had experienced. We thought, 'This is pure gold. If our lives can be changed like this, so can thousands of others.' We wanted to tell the world about Vine & Branches Church and its vibrant pastor, Neil Gentry.

Nicole dove headfirst into the children's program, and I began volunteering at the church coffee shop and with the parking team. It went on like that for a long time and we were so happy. Dixie and Dottie were ecstatic. The more we did at the church, the more friends they made and the more they enjoyed it. They loved being there as often as we found ourselves there, which was a lot. We felt the same way, and we believed we were setting a good example for them. And we saw the good it was doing them. They were happy and they were falling in love with God. What more could we ask for?

After months of serving and getting more and more involved in our respective ministries, Nicole and I began to get noticed. Assistant pastors, elders, and other staff members began to recognize us because we were around so much; they introduced themselves and befriended us. It went on like that for months as we became more and more ingrained in the culture of Vine & Branches.

Eventually, we were invited into the homes of these various leaders and staff members and church people. We were becoming part of what I now call "the inner circle." These were our closest friends and this had become our world. As I reflect on it now, that was an unhealthy place for us to be. I don't think we were spiritually mature enough to understand the balance needed between in-depth church involvement and living in the real world.

That's when we met Spencer Devereux. Late thirties. Single. In excellent physical health. The looks of a Ken doll with dirty blond hair and a five o'clock shadow. From the first night we met Spencer at a big thank you gathering for all of the volunteers at Vine & Branches, something about him did not sit well with me. He struck me as an extremely serious person. All business. Rarely cracked a smile. Always working, working, working. A very focused individual and, seemingly, under a lot of pressure. As I reflect on it now, I believe Spencer was a scout of sorts who was always on the lookout for the volunteers in the church from whom he could get the most mileage—without actually paying them by bringing them on staff.

Spencer was Pastor Neil Gentry's executive assistant, so he was the righthand man. I've come to think of Spencer as the gatekeeper to the throne. That first night we met him, he cornered Nicole and they spoke for a good twenty minutes. When we were getting ready for bed later that night, Nicole told me Spencer had asked her if she would "pray about" becoming the assistant to the person who was in charge of the children's ministry, which, at the time, was an enormous group of kids who were the age of our girls. That group alone included hundreds of children. But the position he was asking Nicole to fill was a volunteer role. The only paid positions were those who headed up the children's program, middle school program, and high school program. Everyone else were volunteers. Dozens of volunteers.

I regret to say that there was something very exciting about cracking the code and making it to the inner circle. Of course, Nicole and I never spoke about it, but to think that we may finally be getting noticed by Pastor Gentry, and possibly even becoming friends with him was exhilarating; he was like a celebrity. We were blinded by his charisma and fame. I'm embarrassed by that now, and regretful.

For the handful of years, we became closer and closer to

Pastor Gentry and those on the inner circle. During that time, Vine & Branches had become a megachurch with thousands of members, multiple services, and a huge staff. The pastor's messages were on TV, radio, and online. He had a huge following on social media. Plus, there were many new churches popping up around the country that were following the Vine & Branches model; Pastor Gentry's sermons were presented live on big screens in many of those churches.

The problem was, the closer and more intertwined we became with that inner circle, the more we were asked to do. It got to a point when Nicole and I were feeling stretched, to say the least. "Frantic" may be a bit strong, but we were definitely feeling pulled in far too many directions. What once had been joyful, heartfelt service toward God had now become legalistic obligation to man.

The more we did at the church, it seemed, the more we were asked to do; almost expected to do! That was wrong. And that ended up being a big part of our downfall.

I had become the head of the coffee shop and of the parking team, so I was responsible for large squads of people, working shifts for four services every Sunday, and for Wednesday night youth programs. It was like having a second full-time job.

Looking back on it, all of the obligations were partially our own fault.

No one forced us to work as hard as we did for the church.

I should have said no.

Nicole should have said no.

But we were young Christians. The thought of "serving" was new to us and, in the beginning, exciting to us—something we *wanted to do*. Pastor Neil would say that true belief in God literally meant obedience, and he stressed—I mean really stressed—that every member should find an area of the church to get "plugged in." That was his mantra: get "plugged in." In other words, to keep this megachurch chugging along, with all its expenses, we all needed to pitch in, serve, and give. Give our time and our money.

Another of Pastor Gentry's favorite mantras he borrowed from the Bible: "Faith without works is dead." Today, it makes me sick to my stomach. In retrospect, the longer we went on, our service and our giving became a rote obligation. We were no longer serving God. Instead, we were serving Spencer Devereux, Pastor Neil Gentry, and the inner circle of the great megachurch.

So, Pastor Gentry was right when he said true belief was lived out through obedience, but he left out the part stating that the obedience should be to God, not to some trumped up narcissists trying to become world famous celebrities.

It's taken me many months, but I've finally figured out what was going on back then. Spencer ran interference for Neil Gentry. Spencer controlled access to the great pastor. And Spencer did more than that. He was the ringleader of a small, powerful group of men who took advantage of people within the congregation of Vine & Branches Church.

These were bad men.

Wolves in sheep's clothing.

They abused the sheep and led them astray.

Because of all the media attention surrounding the alleged financial misconduct within the church and the alleged sexual advances of Pastor Neil Gentry, Vine & Branches has been forced to conduct internal interviews and a thorough "unbiased" investigation. Nicole will be interviewed tomorrow. I fear how that will turn out.

I'm fully convinced the church leaders intend to ride the storm out, put all of the allegations behind them, and continue to grow their megachurch empire.

You see, once men have tasted power, control, and celebrity — the allure of it is insatiable.

They must have it again.

*I can't let that happen.*

# FOUR

**Horace Stone** *(The Washington Post)*: Based on the in-depth information we've gathered and the extensive interviews we've done, it appears Vine & Branches Church had some sort of hierarchy in place that not only insulated Pastor Neil Gentry, but also helped cover up his supposed affairs and possibly even groomed women for him and provided special treatment to those within his inner circle. What more can you share about this?

**Marilyn Mansell** *(Christianity Now Magazine)*: After a man proved himself to be faithful to Pastor Neil Gentry and Vine & Branches Church—and this often took years—then that person may be invited by Pastor Gentry to become an elder of the church. Nothing was brought before the congregation. The elders voted, but remember, the elders were all Pastor Gentry's hand-picked men; women were rarely invited. From what we have found, every one of these men was, for lack of a better term, a groupie of Pastor Gentry. These were his biggest fans. He was an idol to them. Therefore, whatever ideas he presented, whatever he wanted to spend, they would rubber stamp it.

**Stone:** I know a big deal was made of his private jet.

**Mansell:** The Gulfstream, oh yes. And his limousines and chauffeurs and catered parties and expensive clothes and watches, and all the real estate holdings. The things he got away with—and may still get away with—are uncanny. How could all of that happen for so many years? This church has been like his own private company. He's been the ruler and CEO. What he says, goes. He's had the final word, the *only* word. There have been no checks or balances. Of course, now they're being forced to do an internal investigation, but, come on, what does that really mean?

**Stone:** And yet, Neil Gentry is still the senior pastor, the spiritual leader of thousands upon thousands of people.

**Mansell:** Right. An incredible and sobering responsibility.

**Stone:** From what I understand, as you've implied, he could potentially get away with all of the frivolous spending and the use of church funds for personal gain. How is that possible?

**Mansell:** Pastor Neil Gentry is not a stupid person. In fact, he is proving to be incredibly adept at playing the system. I know you're aware how much money Vine & Branches Church brought in during its heyday.

**Stone:** Now that you mention it, two years ago the church had a budget of sixty-six million dollars. They did not provide audited financial statements, only basic financial details. The fiscal year financial overview revealed that the church spent twenty-four million dollars on its weekly services and programs for all ages. Also, four million dollars went to the church's Evening Embers events, and a whopping nineteen million went to its TV, radio, and social media ministry. For general, administrative, and legal expenses, the church used ten million dollars, and another seven million was used for fundraising. The remaining two million was spent on missions and outreach.

**Mansell:** This is a powerful church. The broadcasts of its services are said to have reached an estimated ten million U.S. viewers each week, and millions more around the world. Pastor Neil Gentry, at one time, had twenty-seven million followers on Facebook, Twitter, and Instagram; that's gone down slightly since all of the accusations came to light, but not by much. His books have sold more than seven million copies in the U.S. alone. And, since the church seems to have weathered the storm about its financial wrongdoings, his popularity has started to tick back up.

**Stone:** I know Pastor Gentry is in the midst of building an enormous mansion on Lake Lanier outside of Atlanta, which will have pools and pickle ball courts and saunas and spas. He is also said to have a penthouse condo near Sarasota, Florida, as well as numerous other real estate holdings. How can all this be justified? How can it be legal?

**Mansell:** First of all, he has a full team of lawyers and accountants to whom his church pays big money in order to make everything legal. Secondly, he is paid a very high salary—the exact amount no one seems to know, and he won't convey—and a lot of the luxury items are written off as business expenses. Another thing they cooked up was this megachurch pastor speaker circuit you may have heard about, where Pastor Gentry, for example, would go speak at another megachurch. That host church would write off all of his expenses, including private jet, limos, five-star accommodations, fine dining, first-class entertainment, and on top of that, he would receive a fifteen-to-twenty-thousand-dollar speaker's fee, which they labeled as an honorarium.

**Stone:** Based on what we've said, I understand that the church's inner circle may not object to all of that, but I am shocked that the congregation didn't balk at it.

**Mansell:** They may not have known. When we interviewed Pastor Gentry, he told us Jesus wouldn't want him to reveal how much money he earned or donated. The church's financials lump all of the salaries together, so there is no way to tell how much he is or was paid on an annual basis. The elders know, I'm sure. We also don't know if he has debts. There are some rumors about that but we haven't been able to confirm anything.

**Stone:** But it's obvious he is—one way or another—making millions of dollars. Here is a list of his holdings that we can confirm to date: multi-million-dollar mansion under construction; at least seven other real estate properties (one in Spain); current residence valued at $4.8 million; New York City penthouse; Gulfstream; multiple Rolexes, shoes, suits, and designer clothes worth thousands; Lamborghini; two Teslas; and, don't forget, he owns the Mission Valley Resort meditation ranch outside of Las Vegas.

**Mansell:** It is extraordinary for a pastor to have this kind of wealth and apparent net worth. And what is unbelievable is that he has, thus far, somehow, gotten away with all of it.

**Stone:** Do you really think so?

**Mansell:** Yes! They have not been able to nail him on any of the financial wrongdoing. I'm telling you, his exorbitantly paid team has been able to justify all of it using loophole after loophole. They follow the tax laws. External investigations are lingering on, but it looks like he is through the worst of it and will be acquitted of all the allegations about the financial crimes.

**Stone:** The allegations about sexual harassment are another story, correct?

**Mansell:** Well, not so fast. The church is finally doing its own internal investigation, and the things I'm hearing don't bode so well for the accusers.

**Stone:** Okay, we will get back to that in a moment, but first clarify, if you will, how many accusers there are and how all that started.

**Mansell:** Brenda Vincent, head of the worship ministry, was the very first accuser. She originally went to the elders with accusations that Pastor Gentry came on to her over the course of several years. According to her, this happened on trips, over meals together, and on multiple occasions when he invited her to his home or hotel suite, when his wife was not present. Pastor Gentry vehemently denied this, and the elders ultimately took his side. But that first cry for help from Brenda Vincent is what broke the ground and started rattling the bones in all the other closets and causing other women to come forward.

# FIVE

"For the record, my name is Spencer Devereux, executive assistant to Pastor Neil Gentry." He leaned over the table, adjacent to the other six serious faces, and spoke directly into the mic of the recorder. "I'm here with three elders of Vine & Branches Church: Blair Post, Connor Creed, and Marshall Landow. Also here representing the church is attorney Troy Beamer. Today is August 12, 2024."

The sole woman at the table, Nicole McQue, appeared to be a nervous wreck, because they were there in one of the church conference rooms to interview her. Nicole's estranged husband, Darren, sat next to her. They had come in separate cars and had not talked before the session began. The air between them was obviously cold and strained but, oddly, there they were, together. That is sometimes what crucibles did.

"With us this afternoon is Nicole McQue, former assistant director of the children's ministry at Vine & Branches. That was a voluntary position, for the record."

*"Voluntary." Ha. It was practically a full-time job.*

"Her husband, Darren McQue, is present as well." Devereux didn't look at the couple when he first spoke. Instead, he eyed the other men at the long table, one by one. "This group is conducting an organization-wide investigation into the behavior of the founder and senior pastor of Vine & Branches Church, Neil Gentry."

Devereux was calculated and business-like. His dark blond hair and eyebrows almost matched his black outfit—denim pants and long-sleeved shirt with silver buttons; all the swirly stitching made it look like a cowboy shirt.

Blair Post and Connor Creed looked as if they'd come from work; they wore sport jackets, slacks, and no ties. Marshall Landow and the lawyer, Troy Beamer, were dressed as if they were about to play golf—Dri-FIT slacks and colorful Nike short-sleeved shirts. The men were silent, swiveling in their chairs, rocking, glancing at their phones, and sipping bottled waters.

During the past ten years, Nicole and Darren had grown close to all of the men at the table, with the exception of the attorney.

A distinct, shadowy aura hung in the room, suggesting an "us against them" mentality permeating from the stone-faced church group.

"Nicole, thank you for coming today. For the record, this board has advised you to go directly to Pastor Neil Gentry with your grievances, is that correct?"

The gloves were off. It was nothing Nicole and Darren hadn't expected.

Nicole cleared her throat and leaned forward. "Yes." She wore white slacks and a teal summer top. She also had on a black sweater because the church was always cold. She held several three-by-five-inch index cards in front of her on the table, which were filled with notes to herself in ink.

"And did you do that?" Devereux said.

"Not since I've left the church, no." She fingered the index cards nervously.

"But you have discussed your complaints with Pastor Gentry, is that so?"

Nicole inhaled deeply and sighed. She had tried to prepare for this for weeks. And now it was time. Her hands trembled.

*Keep it simple. Be clear.*

"Toward the end of my time here at the church, on several occasions, I confronted Pastor Gentry with my concerns and his words to me were, 'I will deny everything, Nikki. And who do you suppose they will believe?'"

Darren glared at Devereux, then at each of the elders with what felt like a flame in his eyes.

Devereux glanced at Troy Beamer and looked at the yellow legal pad on the table in front of him. He had avoided eye contact with Darren at all costs. "We are here today to hear your story, Nicole. So, why don't you tell us about your relationship with Pastor Gentry and how things evolved, according to your recollection."

Nicole looked down at the table, locked in, and looked back at Devereux. "His advances toward me started when I became the assistant director of the children's ministry. The church put on a big week-long summer program for kids in the church and in the community. We had a dunking booth." Nicole stopped suddenly and a hand flew to her mouth. She almost cried out loud. But she held it in.

Darren flinched, as if reaching for her, but stopped. She waited with a fist to her mouth. Closed her eyes. Composed herself. "While I was sitting up on the perch, being dunked periodically, Pastor Gentry was watching me in an obvious and uncomfortable way. He stepped right up to the plexiglass and just stared at me with a seductive smile. It was very clear he was wanting my attention."

"And what was your reaction?" Devereux said.

"I, I glanced at him several times to make sure I was seeing what I was seeing, but, for the most part, I looked away and kept laughing with the kids. I honestly couldn't get my head around the fact that he was staring at me."

"For the record, Nicole, do you remember what you were wearing that day?"

Nicole's face flashed hot. Her jaw clenched. She thought and thought. "Denim shorts! And a sweatshirt. And a bra, if that's what you're insinuating, Spencer!" Her heart pounded against her rib cage. How dare they try to flip this on her.

Devereux shook his head with his mouth hanging open and said nothing, apparently caught in his insinuation. Finally, he spoke up. "Was anything said . . . did Pastor Gentry say anything to you that day at the dunking booth?"

"No," Nicole said sharply. "He didn't have to."

Devereux looked around at the other faces with a confident smirk.

Nicole looked down at her cards. "Next was the Anchors Away Back to School Bash," she said. "I was eating with a table full of kids and Pastor Gentry came over and sat with us. He sat right next to me. After making pleasantries with the kids, he turned his focus on me. He told me he liked the way I had my hair that day. It was pulled back and tied behind my head and he said he liked it off of my forehead, that I had a pretty forehead. He told me that often. And pretty eyebrows."

Darren shifted uncomfortably in his chair. Although he'd heard this before, it hit him hard all over again.

"He then turned the conversation to our families and our kids—his and mine—and asked if I was glad they would be back in school soon. I said not really. He said he was glad and that it took a lot of pressure off him and his wife, Becky. He then asked me what I would be doing all day long now that my kids would be back in school. The way he said it, he was implying a hook-up."

All of the elders shifted at the same time.

"Did he *say* that?" Devereux squawked.

"Again, he didn't have to. It was implied in his tone of voice, and the way he looked at me."

"Is that it?"

"For that occasion, yes," Nicole said. "You have to understand, the instances I'm telling you about are only but a few. There were many, many constant long stares, glancing touches, and private comments when he was all-out flirting with me."

"Funny, he told us the same about you," said Blair Post, one of the elders.

Darren started to argue, but Devereux cut him off. "That's not necessary, Blair. We'll get to his side later. Today, we need to hear Nicole out. Please continue. Darren, I'm sorry, but you are not here to speak today."

Nicole examined one of her cards. "Thanksgiving. The turkey giveaway. At the last minute he told me he was going to be riding with me. We had collected all the turkeys and this was the day we were driving them to various neighborhoods. What was I going to say? This was Neil Gentry. I just felt I had to do what he said and let him ride with me."

"Why weren't you and your husband riding together?" Darren fumed.

"He'd taken the girls to his mother's house to celebrate Thanksgiving early."

"And so what do you imply happened?" said the attorney, Troy Beamer.

"Pastor Gentry made fun of my driving. He got all sarcastic like he was scared that we were going to wreck. It was like childish flirtation. After we'd delivered all of our turkeys, he stopped me in the car in the parking lot of the apartment where we were. He put his hand on mine and he said, 'Nicole, I want you to know how thankful I am for you, for your service to the church.' He said something provocative, like, 'Your spirit is contagious.' He squeezed my hand and said, and I quote, 'I want more of you. More than I'm allowed to have.'"

The men at the table all seemed to shift and swivel and clear their throats at the same time.

"And when he was joking, like he does so often, were you laughing?" Devereux said. "Was it funny? Did you laugh along with him?"

Nicole blinked several times, seemingly frustrated. "Some of it was funny, I guess."

"Did you laugh?" Devereux said forcefully.

"Yes."

Devereux nodded. "And when he touched your hand, did you let him? Did you pull your hand away?"

Her head snapped away and she blew a sigh of frustration. "This is the senior pastor of one of the most popular churches in the world. I was shocked. I didn't know what to do. I was scared. I was flabbergasted. I kept thinking, this can't be happening."

"So, you weren't playing along at all, enjoying it," said elder Connor Creed.

"How dare you!" Darren yelled.

"Darren, stop!" Devereux ordered. He looked at Connor and

back at Nicole. "Did you take your hand away, Nicole? Yes or no."

She let out a slight squeal and inhaled shakily as she leaned back in the chair. "After . . . after he said what I told you, about wanting more of me, I did. Yes. I took it away. And I drove us back to the church. Nothing more was said that day."

Troy Beamer and Marshall Landow scribbled notes, perhaps jotting down questions.

Nicole appeared to be concentrating hard on breathing in deeply through her flared nostrils followed by long, silent exhales. Her face looked so different—so taut. Her shoulders and arms were the same, just skin and bones. She had to have lost thirty pounds since the alleged relationship with Pastor Neil Gentry had come to light. Her five-foot-six-inch frame, which was once quite voluptuous, now had the look of a woman suffering from anorexia.

"What else do you have?" Devereux broke the silence.

Nicole sighed. She glanced at the top index card, but it appeared she already had everything memorized. "At the church Christmas party, Pastor Gentry came up to me in the buffet line and whispered that he had a Christmas gift for me; he wanted to give it to me later in the evening. My husband was right next to me, but he was busy talking to someone. Pastor Gentry said this to me with a sensual tone."

Devereux blinked, tilted his head, and shot a look of doubt. "This is all so very subjective, but go on," he said.

"I shook my head and whispered no. I felt guilty and embarrassed. I looked around to see if anyone may have heard, but no one had. I couldn't believe he did this with Darren so nearby. Anyway, after dinner and dessert, he came up to us at our table and said right in front of Darren that he needed to "borrow" me for a few minutes. My face turned red instantly." She glanced at Darren and looked back at Devereux. "I went because, again, this is the leader and founder of this huge organization. How could I say no?"

Connor popped his eyes as if to say, "Simple. You just say no."

Darren moved a pen over his pad slowly, deliberately, recalling that he had indeed felt a tinge of jealousy at that moment during the Christmas party, but that he had discounted it because, after all, this was the great man of God—Pastor Neil Gentry, asking to speak to one of his key volunteers.

"We took the elevator up to his office," Nicole said, staring blankly at a wall. "It was dark, very few lights on. From a drawer in the suite part of his office he produced a small box professionally wrapped in Christmas paper. I was completely uncomfortable. This was—"

"Yet, you were there," blurted Connor, "following him up to his office—at night. Just the two of you."

Devereux held up a hand toward Connor and shook his head for silence.

"You have to understand . . . I trusted him! He was my pastor!"

"Please keep going," Devereux said.

"He insisted I open the package right then, so I did." She glanced at Darren, and hesitated. "It was a necklace with a contemporary silver cross on a small leather disc." Again, she shot an embarrassed look toward Darren. "He put it around my neck. Then he squeezed my neck and rubbed my shoulders."

Everyone was silent. No one moved. It was as if time had stopped.

She had never told Darren the part about the physical touch. He imagined it happening and it hurt him like a scalpel and made his anger boil at the same time. He remembered the necklace. He'd commented how much he liked it the first time he saw her wearing it. He'd even asked her where she'd gotten it. She'd lied and told him eBay, where she did a fair amount of thrifting.

"It was totally inappropriate," Nicole added.

"Then what happened?" Devereux said.

"I was so confused. I was utterly dumbfounded. He had power. I was just . . ."

"Did anything else happen in his office that night?" Devereux said.

"He told me he needed me." Nicole said this looking straight down at the polished table in front of her. "He said I was young and vibrant and . . . irresistible."

Blair sighed audibly and shifted uncomfortably in his chair.

The attorney cleared his throat.

Darren had not heard these details. His hatred for Gentry and these fake leaders and this phony church exploded in his mind. He realized his pen was digging into his legal pad. He smacked the pen down in frustration.

"Anything else?" Devereux said.

"What more do you want?" Darren blurted.

Nicole gave a stern look to each of the elders and then faced Devereux. "He asked if he could kiss me."

The words just hung there in the air of that dark, freezing room.

Darren had not known this. He felt humiliated in front of all those men. He felt betrayed. He had been a complete idiot for not knowing what was going on.

"I was literally in shock," Nicole blurted. "I was confused. This was one of the most influential evangelical leaders in the whole country—hitting on me like a guy in a bar."

"I don't understand what you were so confused about," Marshall said in a tense tone. "If what you say is true and this man was making advances toward you, why didn't you slap him and go tell your husband? Simple solution. Why didn't you do that? Answer us that."

Nicole glared at him in silence, then at the others. Her lips were sealed shut and her eyes were ablaze.

"Think about the context," Nicole said. "Everyone admired this man and his massive church. I did not want to hurt the church, so I just thought, 'I won't tell anyone.' I felt that if I exposed him, this amazing church would crumble.'"

"So, what happened next?" Devereux said, sounding exhausted with it all.

"I left."

"You didn't allow him to kiss you?" Blair said.

"No. I left. I practically ran out. I took the necklace off on the elevator and put it in my purse."

"Can you show us this necklace?" Devereux said.

Darren's heart sunk because he knew the answer already.

Nicole frowned. Her chin dropped to her chest.

"I don't have it."

# SIX

"Neil? Honey? Did you hear me?" Becky Gentry called from what would eventually become the spacious new master bedroom, situated on the main level of the massive home under construction overlooking Lake Lanier. Sunlight streamed in through the open framework all around her.

"Yeah, babe, sorry," Pastor Neil Gentry yelled back. "I took pictures and sent them to Parker. We'll see what he says."

*Good.*

Becky had spotted several pieces of wood in the framing of the master bathroom that appeared to her to be rotted. Parker, the site manager, would take care of it.

She walked on the wood floor over to what would eventually become the large sitting area of the bedroom. It was framed for a huge picture window. She stood there and looked out toward the dark blue, shimmering lake.

Whenever they came out to the home site, there always seemed to be a wonderful breeze, as there was now, which was unusual for Atlanta in August. The huge structure—which was now framed and roofed—sat high above and far away from the other houses dotting the enormous lake. This would truly be a showplace; appropriately, a beacon on a hill. She could already picture it in *People* magazine.

Staring at the rippling water, Becky's stomach flip-flopped

again. She couldn't help but wonder what was going on at the church with Nicole McQue and the elders and attorney. It was the day they were taking her formal statement about Neil. Becky had heard through the grapevine that Nicole's testimony would be some of the most incriminating yet.

Ever since Brenda Vincent, the former worship leader at Vine & Branches, had lied about Neil making sexual advances toward her, a number of others had come out of the woodwork to try the same thing. All wanting to have their name in lights. All wanting to make a quick buck. All jumping on Satan's bandwagon to try to take down the godly man who'd built the church everyone was talking about and copying.

Neil was strong. He was a man of God. A man of faith and morals. A man committed to his wife and children. He would never do the things of which they were accusing him. It was all preposterous.

Becky spun around, ridding herself of the negative thoughts. She envisioned the new comfy chairs and ottoman she'd selected from Pottery Barn for the master sitting area. She and Neil were in the process of selling and giving away much of their old furniture with the intention of getting mostly new things for the lake house.

A floor below where she stood now would be the enormous terrace level (they were determined not to call it a basement) featuring a home theater, billiard table, pinball machines, ping pong table, video game room, and lots of comfy seating for the kids and their friends.

She found Neil, as she so often did, texting away on his phone. He was leaning against the frame of the extra-large island in the kitchen with the sunlight beaming bright beyond the many framed kitchen windows.

"Hey," Becky said.

Neil looked up at her. "Hey. What do you think? They're making good progress, yeah?"

Becky nodded enthusiastically. "Yeah."

"Have you heard from Savannah?" he said.

Savannah was the teenager who was keeping an eye on their two children, Eli and Hazel.

Becky got her phone out and looked. "No, but I'm sure they're fine. Why?"

"Nothing. Will you just check in to be sure," Neil said. "I know they were going to hang out at the pool."

Neil's younger brother, Teddy, had died in a drowning accident when they were teenagers, so he was always concerned when it came to the kids and water, even though Eli and Hazel were proficient swimmers.

"Sure." Becky shot a quick text to Savannah asking how things were going.

"I got a text from Devereux." Neil held up his phone and looked at Becky with a sober stare. "The things she's saying are bad. I'm just gonna warn you."

Becky felt sick instantly. Her head spun slightly. She felt hot. "Like what?"

"She's saying I gave her a necklace as a Christmas present."

Becky's heart plunged.

"She's also saying that I asked if I could kiss her." Neil walked over to Becky and wrapped his arms around her. "Why is this happening?"

Becky hugged him and brought his head to rest against her shoulder. "We're going to make it through this, Neil. This is nothing but the enemy, trying to tear down what we've built. The truth will come out. You know it will."

Neil continued to hold Becky, not saying anything, not looking at her.

Becky did worry about the fallout from the current investigation by the church. What if people actually believed these lying women? Could Neil possibly be fired? Or worse, could he go to prison if the police were to get involved?

She held him closely. He needed her. He was under so much pressure. Vine & Branches was one of the fastest-growing churches in America. God had chosen her to be his helpmate. She was determined to stand strong and to be there for him—especially amidst all the flaming arrows from the evil ones.

"They've tried this before and failed, honey," she said softly. "All of the accusations about the finances. God has you. You're a good man." She patted his head as it rested against her shoulder.

"I hate it for you," he said. "It's so embarrassing. It's humiliating. Sometimes I think we should just pack it in and start new someplace else."

She pulled back from him, he lifted his head, and their eyes met.

"Listen to me, Neil. I can handle this. I don't care what anyone else thinks or says. I trust you. I know you're doing God's work, and Satan hates it. We'll get through this and we'll be stronger than ever."

Her phone buzzed. As she got it out, she felt a stab of concern deep inside. It wasn't just Brenda Vincent and Nicole McQue. There were others. Two others and talk of more. She worried for Eli and Hazel. They were getting old enough to hear things, to understand things, and to question what was going on.

Neil answered a call on his phone the way he always did simply by saying, "Yo, go." He was so busy, pulled in so many directions. She was sorry he had to endure the current firestorm. It wasn't fair.

Becky looked at her phone. The text from Savannah said everything was fine. She and the kids were still swimming but would be going in for lunch soon.

Eli and Hazel had once been best friends with Nicole and Darren McQue's daughters, Dixie and Dottie. They were similar in age and always at the church, so they'd become extremely close. Eli and Hazel asked about seeing the McQue kids almost daily it seemed. That was rough on Neil and her because it served as a constant reminder of the allegations hanging in the air.

It also hurt Becky deeply that Nicole had betrayed her. They had been close friends, all four of them, Neil and Darren, too. That's why it had been such a bombshell when Nicole accused Neil of making sexual advances toward her.

"What do you mean you can't do it?" Neil barked at whoever he was talking to on the phone. "You said it would work. You guaranteed it would fit."

Becky shot him a questioning look.

Neil spun away from her. "Look, Parker, we took you at your word. You said you could make it fit, so you need to figure it out.

It's on you. I'm not a builder, you are. That's what we're paying you for."

Neil turned around, looked at Becky, and seethed.

"What?" Becky mouthed.

He shook his head in disgust. "Hot tub. He says it won't fit now."

"He needs to make it fit," she said.

Everything for the deck was planned and purchased, from the 14-person hot tub to the elegant stonework and waterfall, from the built-in seating and furniture to the fireplace, special lighting, and landscaping.

"Listen to me. We are not choosing a smaller one, Parker. Get that idea out of your head. Make it work. I've got to go." Neil ended the call, took an enormous breath, and stuck his hands on his waist. "It never ends."

"What about the rotten wood?" she said.

"He said it's not bad but he's going to have his guys replace it anyway."

"Good."

*I know rotten wood when I see it.*

# SEVEN

"Let's back up one moment," Spencer Devereux continued leading the questioning of Nicole McQue in the cold, dark conference room at Vine & Branches Church. Present around the long table were the church's three elders and attorney, as well as Nicole's husband, Darren McQue. "Just a quick side-note question, Nicole. I know you said you no longer have the necklace in question. Did you ever wear the necklace that you say Pastor Gentry gave to you?"

The question cold-cocked Nicole.

And it implied she was lying.

She never imagined they would ask such a thing, not in all the worrying and anticipation of this day; it never crossed her mind they would go down that road because any mention of the necklace, in her mind, made Gentry look guilty.

Nicole had considered telling them what had happened to the necklace, to use it as ammunition against Gentry, but only if it appeared necessary to win her case; otherwise she thought it sounded too far-fetched. She had to sound credible and believable —and the story behind what happened to the necklace was neither of those. Plus, she didn't have the necklace; that was the biggest problem.

She must have looked like a deer in headlights.

"Well?" Devereux said.

"Yes . . . I wore it. Only a few times. Simply because it was pretty. It looked good on me. It had no meaning to me."

*That was a lie.*

She couldn't even look at Darren. The humiliation this was putting him through was merciless.

"How many times would you say you wore this so-called necklace?" Devereux pried. "Ten?"

*I can't believe this.*

Nicole blinked and curled her hair behind her right ear.

"A handful. Maybe five at most," she said. "Probably less."

"And didn't you wear it so Pastor Gentry could see it on you?"

Nicole's face warmed—from rage, from guilt. She wanted to crawl under the table.

"I wore it because it looked good on me. That's all."

"So, Pastor Gentry never saw you wearing the necklace he supposedly gave you and commented on it, how good it looked on you?" Devereux said.

*How can I be the one in the wrong here?*

Nicole fumed. "If you want to know the truth, yes, I wore the stupid necklace a few times. He noticed it and flirted with me, like he always did. I cannot believe you are taking his side. He came on to me! One time, in fact, he admired the necklace and felt it, the pendant, and then he patted my chest, my upper chest, right here." She put her right hand on the upper center part of her chest. "This man is a *predator*. And you're trying to spin it to make *me* look like the bad guy. I'm not the bad guy, your pastor is!"

"Please calm down, Nicole. Are you telling us today that you had no part in Pastor Gentry's supposed actions?" Devereux said. "What I mean is, you didn't help trigger his actions in any way? Because, I must say, his recollection of his interactions with you are remarkably different than you are remembering. He told us you are flat-out lying and colluding against him. Could it be you are misremembering?"

"Are you kidding me?" Darren blurted, rising from his seat.

Nicole's face was on fire.

"Pastor Gentry came after me!" Nicole said sternly. "Once he got his sights set on me, he was relentless. None of that was my fault. He initiated all that. But, yes, after a period of time I will say, I got weak. I'm embarrassed to say it, in front of my husband. But this man of power and influence, his advances did impact me. To an extent . . . I fell for it."

"So you *did* have feelings for Pastor Gentry."

"To clarify, this was after months of him pursuing me."

"Were you in love with him?"

Darren practically spun out of his chair.

Nicole said, "If you take this out of context—"

"It is what it is, Nicole. Please answer the question. Were you in love with him?"

She dropped her head and cried and wiped her nose with a tissue.

The answer was probably yes. He'd had her in his spell. And now, looking back on it, it was evil and dirty and despicable. She hated that monster.

"I don't know," Nicole finally said. "But he said he was in love with me. And I never said that to him."

The attorney drew in a deep breath and several of the elders murmured.

Devereux huffed and smirked. "This is really, I must say, this is . . . Let's put it this way. You can see how this could easily appear to look as if you were pursuing Pastor Gentry."

Nicole and Darren erupted at the same time, but Devereux half stood and held up both hands, ordering them to back down.

"What I'm saying is," Devereux spoke over them, "we have two opposite stories coming out here. It is extremely concerning. But let's do this, let's finish this up, about the necklace, because there are other things we need to cover. Where is the necklace, Nicole?"

Her face fell and her shoulders slumped.

She would have to go there after all.

*They won't believe me.*

"This will be out of order," Nicole said. "I was telling you what happened in order, in sequence."

Devereux frowned and gave a condescending wave. "It doesn't matter. We need to finish up with the necklace and move on. So I want to bring closure on the necklace. Where is it now?"

"Okay, well, I don't want to rush this," Nicole said.

"Go on."

"When I confronted Gentry about—"

"*Pastor* Gentry," injected Blair Post.

Nicole glared at him. "There came a time when I became overwhelmed by the whole thing. I was consumed by guilt. I was having panic attacks. I knew what was happening was wrong and I literally woke up one day and said, 'Enough.' I wanted it to end. I deleted every text and email from him. Now I know that was a mistake. I regret it.

"Anyway, I went to his office and asked to see him. He let me in right away and I told him it had to end. At first, he was civil. He told me to calm down and we would talk through it. But then he got emotional. He said it would break his heart if we ended it. He said I was all he had to look forward to."

That was a bombshell.

Everyone in the room was on edge, breathless.

"I was determined. I stood my ground. And then, all of the sudden, he got angry because he wasn't getting his way. It was like Jekyll and Hyde."

Nicole's breathing hitched. She wiped her nose with the tissue and set her resolve, just like she had that day she was describing.

"He began to insist that we could not end it. And he said if I did stop, that he would make my life miserable. He told me he would make it look like I had been pursuing him, and he said everyone would take his side. He said, between him and the elders, they could ruin me and my family. He knew how plugged in we were. He knew we'd built our lives around this church. He said he would make us outcasts. He got furious. I couldn't believe it. I was in shock. As I stood my ground, he faked throwing a big glass bookend at me. He grabbed my shoulders and shook me."

"That is such a lie!" Landow blurted. "Why are you doing this, Nicole?"

"Shut up, Marshall!" Darren yelled. "Let her finish."

"Ridiculous," Connor murmured.

"Does this pertain to the necklace, Nicole?" Devereux said. "Because, if not . . ."

"Yes! He grabbed it and ripped it off my neck."

Devereux buried his head in his hands on the table and the others threw themselves back in their chairs disgustedly.

"He kept it," Nicole said. "He told me to get out. He said he would deny everything and no one would believe me. He said if I wasn't silent, he would make me look like a lying psychopath."

"With good reason!" declared Blair Post.

"Do you have any pictures of the necklace, of you wearing the necklace?" Devereux said. "Or did anyone see you wearing it who could attest to it?"

"I saw it." Darren leaned forward and set his elbows on the table and rested his chin on his clasped hands. "She had it on one day and I complimented her on it. She told me she got it on eBay."

Devereux and Landow shook their heads in silence.

*They don't believe me. They're taking his side.*

"For the record, before we move on," Devereux said, "Pastor Gentry vehemently denies that there was ever any necklace."

"Yeah, that's because he's doing exactly what he told me he was going to do—make me out to be some kind of devious lunatic. He has that necklace."

# EIGHT

Devina Jo Hawkins leaned over the bathroom sink in her vast high-rise condo, an expensive two-bedroom that overlooked manicured landscaping, a rooftop swimming pool, and a vanishing edge waterfall. Beyond that was the lush green wooded landscape of Midtown Atlanta, which, from way up there, resembled a field of broccoli with an occasional skyscraper poking through, straight up into the clouds.

Having grown up in a shotgun shack on Monroe Street in Stone Mountain, Georgia, Devina never dreamed she would live in such an expensive place.

Now it was home.

She did her lipstick just the way Saul liked it, thick and dark pink. She'd had her eyes and lashes done at the place around the corner, which she never could have afforded two years ago. She picked up the fancy bottle of House of Sillage Love is in the Air Limited Edition and sprayed it on generously here and there and everywhere. After Saul had given it to her she looked up the perfume online and was flabbergasted to learn it was over $1,200 a bottle.

She stepped back from the mirror and examined herself. Looking good, but she still needed earrings and a full-length view, so she clicked her heels out to the sprawling master bedroom where mirrors surrounded her, as did thick white carpet.

At her big, velvet jewelry box she chose a pair of large silver hoop earrings. She put them on, stepped back, and examined herself in the mirrors. The tight white summer dress looked dazzling against the contrast of her brown skin, even better than it had looked in the store at Phipps Plaza. *Mama and Daddy would definitely not approve.* The heels were shiny white and high, too high, but that's what Saul insisted upon.

"Alexa, turn it up," Devina called toward the kitchen as she swooped up her tall glass of Sauvignon Blanc and headed in that direction. "Alexa, turn it up more," she yelled. The deep bass, smooth jazz sound of Kim Waters filled the plush condo like an incoming tide.

*Yeah.*

She admired the beautiful large living room with its luxurious white, beige, and ivory furnishings and wall décor; a stunning collection of soft leather and white-washed wood that Saul had insisted upon purchasing for her. In fact, he'd footed the bill for a personal consultation with one of Atlanta's most well-known interior designers, Fong Tao, who had asked Devina a slew of questions, then proceeded to fill the place with the magnificent furnishings that surrounded her now.

*It's almost too good to be true.*

In fact, she superstitiously believed if she thought about it too much, it would all vanish as quickly as it had come.

Atlanta's late afternoon sun flooded the condo. It was a tad warm. Devina went over and tapped the thermostat down to sixty-five, relishing the fact that she didn't have to worry about any expenses; Saul took care of everything. That meant not only the mortgage and utilities, but clothes, food, and transportation.

She swayed to the music as she made her way into the kitchen, with the screen of the Echo Show swiveling to follow her. The bottle of wine was still out, and she filled her glass up halfway. Saul's driver would be there soon.

Saul was a busy and important man, and obviously extremely successful. His last name was Dagon, pronounced like 'wagon' but with a D, he always said. He was in the oil industry, based in Texas. She guessed him to be about forty-five, but never asked. That's because she viewed her role as that of a fun friend and upbeat playmate. When he came to town, he wanted to blow off some steam, to relax and enjoy himself. He always said he wanted to forget about work and simply unwind and enjoy some of the 'fruits of his labors.' He took her out to all the finest restaurants, clubs, and shows—the kind most people couldn't afford. Exclusive places. Places she never even knew existed.

From the very first time she'd met Saul in the Publix grocery store where she used to work in the flower department, their relationship had been pleasurable and exciting. He had been buying a big bouquet for a client. They had struck up a light conversation. He was all dressed up in a dark suit and no wedding ring. Although Devina was much younger, he'd asked if she might like to go out for a nice dinner "in the city," the next time he returned to Atlanta. She'd shyly given him her number thinking she would never hear from him again.

When Saul finally returned to Atlanta several weeks later, he called Devina and asked her out to dinner. A limousine had picked her up and whisked her to Quartz, a five-star eatery in Tuxedo Park. Saul met her there. He was casual and breezy. Free and easy. No ties or commitments. He never asked about her age or past relationships, or about her family, and she had the feeling he did not want her to ask about any of those things, either. Saul seemed to be a private person; at least, when they were together he wanted to blend in, kind of be anonymous. He was generous. He lived in the present tense, in the moment. He didn't seem interested in rehashing the past or worrying about the future.

After their fourth fancy outing together, Saul had asked Devina if she would like to stay over at his hotel. He said he had a penthouse suite and that he would make it worth her while. But, no pressure, no pressure.

Well, Devina was no escort. But she found Saul quite attractive, for an older man. And she was at a place in her life—having dropped out of college and working at a supermarket chain—that she needed to find out what the wealthy man had meant when he'd said, "make it worth your while."

Although she'd found the overnight experience awkward and somewhat strange, the twelve crisp one hundred dollar bills she'd found in her shoe early the next morning had been more than enough to cover any misgivings she may have had.

Several weeks after that night, Saul phoned Devina from his home in Texas. He told her a current new business venture was going to be bringing him to Atlanta more frequently in the coming months and years, so he was thinking about investing in a condo in Midtown. He wanted to know if Devina would be interested in decorating the place and actually living there, free of charge. He would stay when he came to town.

She was bowled over.

Of course, he had no idea where she had lived, in a cockroach infested dump of an apartment in Stone Mountain, where the landlord never made any improvements and failed to fix anything that broke. In fact, Devina didn't think Saul had a clue about the type of life from which he'd delivered her.

So, in Devina's mind, if she could simply continue playing the part of the pretty, fancy, fun, easygoing young woman Saul had befriended, life could go on this way indefinitely.

She sipped her wine and checked her watch, but something nagged at her.

"Alexa," she snapped.

The robot-like device swiveled toward her.

"Turn it off."

The music stopped.

It was that hollow, homesick feeling again.

She leaned against the large kitchen island and sighed.

Saul would be spending the night. He would obviously expect things . . .

*You're an expensive hooker. A whore. You know that.*

Saul was using her. Buying her.

He did not love her.

*What would Mama and Daddy think?*

They would tell her how wrong it was—in God's eyes. And deep down she knew that was true.

*No. Don't think about it.*

Saul would be up in the night, padding around in his bare feet, standing out on the balcony, searching his phone, unable to sleep.

Things weren't as good for him as he portrayed.

*This is not real, this lifestyle. None of it is real. He has problems you know nothing about.*

Saul would leave cash. *He always does.* Lots of it. In addition to all this . . .

Devina looked around at the lavish surroundings. The beauty. The comfort.

Saul even paid for a maid.

She thought of her filthy apartment in Stone Mountain, the bugs, not having enough money to buy a measly fast-food hamburger.

*You can't give this up.*

She had to keep going, to keep playing the game.

She checked her phone to see how far out the driver was.

Four minutes.

*Good.*

She needed to go.

*Forget all this . . . guilt.*

She threw back the last of the wine.

*Ah.*

There was more of that where she was going. And perhaps a nice ribeye . . .

# NINE

As Darren McQue sat restlessly in the swivel chair in the dark church conference room, watching his wife Nicole give her testimony—and get grilled by Spencer Devereux and the elders and attorney—he sadly doubted his marriage was going to weather this storm.

Nicole had obviously had feelings for Neil Gentry that had lasted months. Darren still wasn't sure how far the affair had gone, but in his mind, his vows with Nicole had been broken. He was going to have an extremely difficult time trusting her again, and he couldn't imagine being intimate with her again. Not only that, but the story had been picked up by *The Washington Post* and other national media, making the whole thing a complete humiliation for him and the girls.

The bald, bulldog attorney Troy Beamer leaned over and whispered something to Spencer Devereux, who then nodded, cleared his throat, and said, "Nicole, let's go back to the supposed text messages and emails."

The jerks had done that the whole time, used words like "supposed" and "alleged," making it sound as if Nicole had a loose screw and had made everything up.

"There's nothing more to say," Nicole said. "When I decided it had to end, I deleted everything, all the texts and emails. I realize now that having those would prove everything I'm saying, but I just wanted to erase it all. I wanted to get back to my real life."

"For the record, Nicole, our IT people have checked all of Pastor Gentry's emails, text messages, and computer files," said Troy Beamer, "and there is nothing—not one communication to or from you."

Nicole laughed sarcastically. "Of course not. That's because he has his own private computer server, which you elders had set up for him. He also has like five phones, at least. You have insulated him to the point where he can do whatever he wants. I'm not the only one. Others have come forward and more will."

"We're not getting into anyone but you in this meeting," said Devereux.

"It's not just the sexual advances, you know. Pastor Gentry is mentally abusive toward anyone who threatens him or his ministry. He is aggressive and controlling." Nicole's voice cracked with emotion. "He'll do whatever he needs to in order to maintain his popularity and status, and the growth of his . . . kingdom. It's a works mentality. We work for free and he makes millions. What's his salary, anyway?"

"That is not what this is about," Devereux said. "You obviously have an axe to grind. Frankly, I'm having a difficult time understanding why you didn't just leave the church."

"When will it be about that?" Darren blurted, unable to contain himself any longer. "What about Fred Canno? When is *that* ever going to get addressed? You guys are letting this prima donna get away with murder. You're nothing but yes men. This man needs to be exposed."

"Darren, we let you be in here at Nicole's request," Devereux said flatly. "We didn't have to do that. We are interviewing Nicole, not you. You seriously need to be quiet or you're out."

"But what about Fred Canno? Seriously," Nicole said. "Here was a godly man, an amazing teacher, who wanted to have an outreach for people outside the church. A Bible study for homeless and addicted men."

"We are not doing this, Nicole!" Devereux arose from his chair. His face was crimson.

"Fred Canno was scorned by Neil Gentry," Nicole's voice rose with emotion, "simply because he wanted to put his energy and affection into a ministry outside the walls of the church. But that couldn't happen because it didn't benefit Gentry's church — and it threatened him."

"Ha!" Connor Creed bellowed. "This is absurd. How long do we have to listen to this?"

Darren's face burned with anger and he said boldly, "Fred Canno was bullied and manipulated by Gentry to the point of having a mental breakdown! There is an underlying culture of bullying and fear in this church and it comes straight from the top. Wake up!"

Devereux shot to his feet and shoved his chair back so hard it cracked the credenza. "You're out of here, Darren." His lanky right arm straightened into an iron arrow pointing directly toward the door.

Darren's stomach flopped and he instantly regretted his outburst. "I won't say any more. I'm sorry."

"Get out, now!" Blair Post pushed his chair back and stood, ready to escort Darren if need be.

Darren was about to try again, but Marshall Landow shoved his chair back and stood.

Connor Creed followed.

They looked like henchmen, standing over Darren as if ready to drag him out behind a shed.

Darren turned to Nicole, who was staring at him with watery eyes, shaking her head ever so slightly. She looked embarrassed and sorry.

He stood and gathered his things with trembling hands.

The room was silent and all eyes were on Darren.

He walked slowly toward the door feeling dizzy.

He took one last glance at the three elders, who were still standing, glaring at him.

"This is so wrong," Darren said. "God knows what's going on. He sees everything. This will not prosper."

The men stepped toward him, but he continued toward the door.

He took one last glance at Nicole.

She mouthed the words, "I'm sorry."

And Darren was gone.

So gone.

So done with this church and these crooks.

Down the bright hallway he went. Fast.

Down the stairs instead of waiting for the elevator.

Through the enormous lobby and atrium and worldly façade.

Bang go the doors. Into the bright light and absorbing heat.

Toward his car, telling himself not to do what he was about to do.

# TEN

**Horace Stone (*The Washington Post*):** Fred Canno. You are sixty-two years old, married to wife Norma for thirty-seven years. A native of Atlanta, which is somewhat rare, and currently a resident of Franklin County, Georgia. You were an elder at Vine & Branches Church for a little over two years, but you attended the church for three years prior to that, so you were there five-plus years in all. Something about the church was obviously appealing to you, let's start with that.

**Fred Canno (former elder, Vine & Branches Church):** I was out of work. I'd been a foreman in a machine shop in Grove City for fourteen years. Got laid off out of the blue. Because of my age, I couldn't find another job. After two months, Norma had to find work. She did so at Dollar General. Very low pay. I started driving a school bus just to make ends meet. As time went on, we were hurting. Plus, I have high blood pressure and some other health-related issues, so all the appointments and meds got expensive. We were burning through our savings, just torching it.

Anyway, some folks from Vine & Branches Church showed up on our doorstep the week of Thanksgiving and brought us a nice turkey. We weren't going to have any. We'd decided, let's just skip it this year, or just get a roasted chicken from Costco for five bucks, something like that. So, they showed up with that and they were the nicest people, a sweet couple and three kids. Somehow, they'd heard about our circumstances.

We were so floored by the gesture that we went to church there that Sunday after Thanksgiving. We fell in love with it. The music was a bit loud, but the people were outgoing toward us, they were happy. The sermon messages by Pastor Gentry were inspiring, challenging. We hadn't been to church in ages. Norma grew up Catholic. My folks only took me at Easter and Christmas. So, Vine & Branches was this exciting, dynamic place—full of love and joy. We decided we wanted to be part of it.

**Stone:** We'll come back to the Thanksgiving outreach in a minute. So, I know you and Norma really dove in and got involved right away.

**Canno:** Oh, yes.

**Stone:** She helped with the nursery. You opened your home up for some type of mid-week small group gathering?

**Canno:** That's right. They call them community groups. We hosted that pretty much the whole time we were there.

**Stone:** Would you call that a Bible study?

**Canno:** Yes. We hosted and one of the elders, Connor Creed, led the Bible study, usually. If he couldn't be there, they eventually let me do it. That's how I fell in love with it and got the idea to start a Bible study for homeless men in the community, many of whom are addicted to drugs and alcohol.

**Stone:** Okay, we'll touch more on that Bible study you hoped to have in a minute. From what you described, Vine & Branches was a vibrant place to be.

**Canno:** Indeed, it was. Pastor Gentry's sermons were uplifting. We would have other pastors from large churches around the country come speak, as well as community leaders. They all seemed to respect and admire Pastor Gentry a great deal. The church was bursting at the seams. It was unbelievable. The energy in that place was contagious.

**Stone:** But something was happening, something was changing. You were losing confidence in Pastor Gentry, were you not?

**Canno:** That took a while. I was 100 percent committed those first few years. It wasn't until I became an elder that I started to . . . question some things.

**Stone:** Like what, specifically?

**Canno:** The way he delegated. I mean, it got to a point where he was delegating everything. When we first got to the church, I felt like he led by example. He visited people in the hospital, he attended leadership meetings. He rolled up his sleeves and got to work. He did a lot. But by the time I became an elder, I began noticing that nothing fell on his plate anymore. All these things came up that needed to be done and it was like, 'We need Bob to do that. We'll get Sue to do that. Ryan can do that.' It was like, that became his job, to delegate everything — then he'd go whistling off to the coffee shop, or to his new property, or to a fancy lunch with a big donor. It all got to his head. He had parking spots reserved just for him at all the campuses. He would arrive late to meetings and leave early. And when something went wrong, he was never to blame, it was always the fault of the volunteers or staff members to whom he had delegated that thing. He blamed everyone but himself.

**Stone:** What else did you begin to notice once you became an elder?

**Canno:** He had anger issues. He'd become arrogant. If anyone ever challenged him, he would become furious because he wanted to control things. Personnel changes were made that didn't make sense to me. Pastor Gentry let go of his secretary — who'd been at the church for many years — and hired a new one, Wendy. Much younger, much less friendly. But much prettier. Her primary job, it seemed, was to keep people away from him. She was given the authority and knowledge to answer virtually any question people may have so he didn't have to be bothered. Another odd one was when the youth pastor left abruptly. The youth group was growing fine, in my opinion, but Gentry felt it had stagnated and that families were leaving because of it. A good number of staff people were leaving, some without saying a word; they just wouldn't be there the next week.

**Stone:** Were severance packages provided to staff members who were let go?

**Canno:** Yes, but to get the severance they each had to sign a non-disclosure agreement.

**Stone:** For what reason? Those are usually given to people leaving corporations for the purpose of keeping sensitive information confidential.

**Canno:** Exactly. This is something Pastor Gentry instituted. Even if you were just volunteering at the church you had to sign a non-disclosure agreement pledging to protect the confidentiality of all information about the church's business operations, staff, volunteers, and guests. At first, I thought he did it because he thought other churches might try to steal his secrets for church growth. But now I believe it was his own behavior he was trying to keep covered up.

**Stone:** That is damning.

**Canno:** Well, I'm trying to call a spade a spade.

**Stone:** Once you got a taste of teaching the Bible study in your home, you wanted to start one in Grove City for homeless and addicted men. Explain what happened with that.

**Canno:** *(sighs)* He shot it down. And he didn't give me a reason. He just said that wasn't something the church needed to do at the time. Period. That was the end of it. I tried to talk to him. I said this would be an outreach in the community, just like when we give away the turkeys at Thanksgiving. He said, no, that wasn't the same thing at all. I've since come to believe the turkeys are a PR stunt to get families to start coming to the church, like we did. But a Bible study for the homeless—what can those people add or give to the church? You see, it's all about the growth of the church. That's all that matters.

**Stone:** It sounds like you and he were becoming conflicted.

**Canno:** Yes. Because I was not going along with his program anymore. Frankly, because I'm older, I really don't think he felt he needed me around any longer. I started to stand up to him and say what I thought. He'd begun to break appointments with people and he was often too busy to attend our meetings. And, for that reason, the meetings meant nothing. We were just spinning our wheels, because nothing got done unless it was approved by him. And it was becoming more and more difficult for us church leaders to get together with him to discuss anything. He was constantly away from the office and his new secretary always covered for him; she became a pro at that. I could never get a meeting with him.

**Stone:** Did Pastor Gentry travel a lot?

**Canno:** Oh my word, yes. He was always gone, speaking at other megachurches and corporations, doing book signings, taking time away for 'reflection and devotions', playing golf, TV appearances, jet-setting around like a celebrity. He said he needed to do all those things for the benefit of the church. He was building the brand, he said. Pfft. You can only pull the wool over my eyes for so long.

**Stone:** Were others starting to feel like you were?

**Canno:** No. Absolutely not. They believed he was doing what was best for the church. They believed everything he said. He was a busy man. And he was our leader. We were lucky to have him. They worshipped the ground he walked on. And he was getting more and more carried away with himself. One of my retired buddies works part-time out at Jones Bridge Country Club. He says Gentry is out there twice a week playing golf and hobnobbing with the country club elites. Believe me, it wasn't like that when we started going to his church. He was always around, always available. He genuinely cared back then. The power and popularity have gotten to him, changed him. It's sad, in my opinion. Sad.

**Stone:** How did it come to a head with you and Pastor Gentry? What made you walk away?

**Canno:** I started getting migraines. It was the weirdest thing. I was really stressed and pressured to say something in front of him and the elders—about the things I was seeing in his behavior. I felt it was my duty as an elder. So when he finally showed up at the shepherd team meeting, I spoke my piece. I said he had become proud, he was not giving his sermons or our church the attention they deserved, he lacked humility, and he had become a bully and a manipulator.

**Stone:** Wow. How did that go over?

**Canno:** *(shakes his head repeatedly)* It didn't. And he didn't even have to say a word. The elders denied it all and stood up for him while he sat back in his chair and smirked at me. I was the one in the wrong. They portrayed me as a jealous wannabe pastor. *(laughs)* Being a pastor is the farthest thing from my mind. They wanted me to sign a non-disclosure agreement.

**Stone:** Did you?

**Canno:** Pfft. What do you think? No. They had nothing on me. I was not an employee. They couldn't bribe me by threatening to withhold a severance package. I knew what I knew in my heart. This man was not lining up with the scriptural description of a genuine, loving, temperate, humble man of God. Where was the goodness and gentleness, the kindness and peace? When I first met Pastor Gentry almost six years ago, he had those traits . . . not anymore. I don't mean to judge, but we are talking about a huge congregation, thousands of people who are giving their hard-earned money—millions upon millions of dollars—to his church. They are trusting the church to be good stewards of their money. But where is that money going? My advice to you is—follow the money. See where it goes.

**Stone:** What are your thoughts about the women coming forward and the allegations being leveled against Pastor Gentry?

**Canno:** *(long pause)* First, I feel sorry for his wife, Becky, and the children. It's a sad state of affairs. I obviously don't know the details of what transpired with each of these women, but I do believe Pastor Gentry needs to be held accountable in each case. I know the church is conducting its own investigation, but if I were these women, I would go to the police. The local prosecutors can't pursue a case unless a crime is reported to law enforcement. However, from what I understand, it can be very difficult to gain enough substantial evidence against someone like Gentry. The standard of proof for bringing a sexual harassment case to the courtroom is extremely high. We're just going to have to see how it plays out. But my concern is, as was so often the case when I was an elder, it looks as if Pastor Gentry may land on his feet, get his way, and be back in the limelight soon. He's like a cat with nine lives.

# ELEVEN

BY THE TIME Becky Gentry returned home late that afternoon, Eli and Hazel were crashed out on the huge sectional sofa in the media room with *The Marvels* playing on the large wall-mounted TV. The ceiling fan was blowing down on them and a large basket of popcorn sat between them. Savannah said they'd worn themselves out at the pool. They'd had a late lunch and the sun-drenched kids had drifted off to sleep about fifteen minutes ago.

Becky recalled how long Savannah had been there, did the math in her head, and dug cash from her purse at the enormous kitchen island. She handed the money to Savannah. "Thank you for being so dependable."

Savannah took the cash and looked at it. "Mrs. Gentry, that's too much. Really. I can't take all that."

Becky shook her head and pushed Savannah's hands away. "You deserve every penny. And I'm going to be contacting you again soon. We've got a lot coming up."

Savannah thanked her again and saw her way out.

Neil had insisted on paying Savannah in the range of thirty to forty dollars an hour because he said he wanted her to be committed to them before anyone else when they needed her. Becky wasn't positive exactly where her cash allowance came from. Each month, Neil gave her at least a thousand dollars cash to be used for things like paying Savannah, going to the movies, ice cream treats, and paying for dinners when Neil was away. Whether the money came from Neil's salary or from church funds was a gray area. It wasn't Becky's job to worry about the source.

She walked to the window overlooking the large, fenced-in back yard and pool, and relished the quiet, hoping the kids would sleep until dinner. This property, too, was a showplace, Becky thought. The thick green fescue lawn was manicured and surrounded by beautiful flowers, rocks, and plants—all watered on timers by a sophisticated irrigation system.

She snickered to herself remembering their first small home in Gwinnett County. It had been a three-bedroom ranch with mauve colored carpet, where all the neighbors were right on top of each other. Neil used to cut the grass and do everything himself back then. That tiny neighborhood was now overwhelmed by encroaching commercial development, as was so much of Metro Atlanta.

They'd moved from house to house, each one bigger and more expensive than the last, and eventually moved into this large estate about four years ago. It was a gated community and somewhat exclusive, but there was really no escaping Atlanta's ever-changing urban sprawl. Now, with the new lake home going up, they had their sights set much higher. The lake house would be much quieter and far-removed from the fast-track roads of Atlanta. Who knew, they may eventually sell this place and make the lake house their full-time home.

*It's going to happen.*

She intended to see to that.

She had that kind of influence over Neil.

And, after all, Neil was at a point now where he could work from anywhere. He answered to no one. He made his own hours. And he deserved that freedom. They both did. They'd shed blood, sweat, and tears for the church over the years. It wasn't like any typical nine-to-five job. They were on call at all hours for the people of the church. Weddings, funerals, hospital visits, endless activities at the church.

Well, they used to do those things. Now, the elders and deacons, and the full-time staff and volunteers took care of most of that. If it was a major donor, Neil would set everything aside and go, of course. But otherwise, there were people in place to handle most anything that was church-related. That's the way it had to be with a brand as big as Vine & Branches.

Becky's phone buzzed. She looked at the screen; it was Neil calling—the picture of him on the beach with the kids at Captiva Island, one of their favorite spots.

"Hey honey," she answered quietly so not to wake the kids.

"Hey babe. How's it going?" Neil said.

"Good. The kids are crashed out. They got a lot of sun today. I'm hoping they sleep till dinner."

"Oh, that's good, that's good. Listen, I've got to meet Ron Sawyer for dinner." It sounded as if Neil was driving. "I'm sorry. He's all hot and bothered, something about the budget. I'll probably be late."

Becky's heart sank. Another night apart.

Ron Sawyer and his wife Jan were among the top givers in the church. They were wonderful people, extremely involved, and genuinely concerned about the welfare of Vine & Branches. When they called, Neil dropped everything.

"Can't you do it during the day?" Becky said. "He did this before. Last minute dinner. He needs to respect your evenings."

"I know, I know. I'll tell him that. But I've already accepted for tonight."

It would be another night of just her and the kids.

"Where're you going?" Becky said, slightly jealous.

"Ah . . . he's gonna let me know."

She paused. "Okay. But you're going to be all mine tomorrow night. Maybe we can go out. I need some time alone with you. I can get Savannah lined up to sit."

Neil rode in silence for a moment, as if he was not paying attention.

"Neil?"

"Yeah, yeah, for sure."

It upset her that he was so distant, so often.

She had to remind herself how busy he was, how important and in demand. They were no ordinary couple. Some statistics, the most reliable ones, noted their church was in the top twenty of the fastest-growing churches in America. It often felt more like a corporation than a church. It was a lot on Neil. But sometimes she wondered if he realized how much pressure was on her as well.

"Give the kids a hug and a kiss," he said. "And don't wait up. You know how Ron is. He'll talk till they close."

When he said that, it often meant he wouldn't show up until two or three in the morning, which she never understood. It's not like they were out partying.

"How late will you be?" Becky asked.

"As late as it takes to appease Ron. You know how he is. He goes on and on."

She shook it off in frustration.

"Have you heard any more from Devereux—about today?" she said.

For a moment, all she could hear on the other end of the phone was the sound of the car gliding down the road.

"They threw Darren out," Neil said flatly.

*Oh* . . . Becky could only imagine the scene.

"The topic of Fred Canno came up. Darren spoke out of turn, saying we have a culture of 'fear, lies, and bullying.'"

"No." Becky was stunned.

"Yes."

"Why?" Becky pleaded. "Why are these people so against us? I don't understand. Darren and Nicole were our best friends." She covered the phone and cried, not wanting Neil to hear her. She'd loved Nicole and Darren, and their girls. They had been so close; like family.

"They're jealous," Neil blurted. "That has to be it. They want the popularity we have. They want to be noticed like we are. It's sick. It really is. It's the enemy, trying to knock us off course. Trying to take our church down."

Becky couldn't help it; she was sobbing now. She had never cried about the broken relationship with the McQues, and now the floodgates opened. She was finally mourning the painful loss.

The line was silent and Becky was afraid Neil had heard her blubbering.

"Don't cry, baby," Neil said. "It's all lies. The truth is going to prevail."

*Could there be some truth to Nicole's accusations?*

*The McQues were such good people.*
*They wouldn't make these things up — would they?*

She refused to even think about what she had hidden in her dresser drawer.

"Remember our verse, honey," Neil came back on. "'On this rock I will build my church and the gates of hell will not overcome it.' We need to cling to that now. Come on. Are you with me?"

But she *did* think of what was in that drawer.

Something she found in a pants pocket of Neil's.

"Honey?" Neil said. "Are you with me?"

Becky stopped herself from doubting and turned her thoughts to the new lake house, the fine automobiles, the private schools, the clothes, the trips, the Ivy League colleges.

"I'm with you," she mumbled.

"That's my girl."

# TWELVE

Everyone in the tight church conference room was fatigued and antsy. They'd been there much of the day. They shifted in their chairs, stretched, and even stood up, paced, picked at the basket of snacks on the side table, and sat back down with quiet sighs and groans.

But Devereux remained firm in his seat, shoulders back, looking fresh as a flower, perusing his notes like an attorney at trial.

Nicole was mentally spent, but she had to remain strong. She took deep breaths. She prayed silently. She read her notes over and over again.

"Okay everyone, I know it's late, but we're almost finished," Devereux said. "I think we'd all rather get this over with today than have to come back tomorrow."

It seemed like the tenth time he'd said that.

He tapped his pad and studied Nicole before speaking. Finally, he said, "Nicole, tell us about the event you say happened at The Hilltop Retreat Center in the North Georgia Mountains."

She knew it was coming, but it still took her breath away.

She was thankful Darren was no longer in the room to hear what was coming.

*At least Darren supported me. Maybe there is hope for us.*

But then again, she knew Darren's personality and she knew

he would have an extremely difficult time overcoming what had happened with Neil Gentry.

"Nicole . . ."

"Yes, sorry." She looked at her notecards and realized her hands were trembling noticeably. She flattened the cards on the table like she was ironing a piece of fabric and clasped her freezing hands in her lap below the surface of the table.

"This was after everything," Nicole said, then cleared her throat. "This was at the most recent staff retreat, after the argument when he took the necklace back and I told him it was over."

There was an uncomfortable pause.

Her brain was fried. She was struggling for how to say it.

"Continue, please," the attorney said, sounding like he wanted to get home for dinner.

"Gentry found me Saturday morning out on the large back patio at the retreat center. I was having my breakfast, reading. Other people were around—people from our church and other guests. He pulled up a chair and sat down. There was no small talk. He said he couldn't live without me. He said I had to let him back into my life, or else."

"Or else what?" Devereux said in an exhausted tone.

Nicole paused. She wanted her next words to have the impact of a bomb.

"Or else he would kill himself."

There was a blur of motion.

Each man at the table recoiled.

Someone cursed. Several laughed in frustration and mockery. Marshall Landow pointed a crooked finger at her and said, "How dare you!"

"Quiet everyone . . . Are you aware what Pastor Gentry said about the weekend retreat at The Hilltop?" Devereux said.

"No," Nicole said bluntly. "But I can imagine."

"He said you insisted he meet you at breakfast that day—"

"That was his alibi for being seen with me," she said. "Go on."

"And that you are the one who threatened to harm yourself if he didn't have a relationship with you."

"Ha. I would never say such a thing. So it's the great pastor's word against mine. Have you ever asked yourselves why I would do this? Why would I make this up? To what end? To ruin my marriage and destroy my own family?"

"This is the stuff of national headlines, Nicole," blurted Connor Creed. "This will put your name in the national media spotlight. I personally believe, to answer your question, *that* is why you're doing this."

"You know what, shame on you, Connor. You are so blind. All of you are blind! Your celebrity pastor is a wolf in sheep's clothing and you don't even know it! Could you be any less discerning?"

Her heart was hammering so hard she thought they may be able to see it thumping through her sweater.

"You're just a bunch of yes men. No one has the guts to stand up to this . . . predator."

"Ha! Predator. Listen to you," said Blair Post, condescendingly. "This really is pathetic." He looked at his watch. "How much longer are we going to listen to this, Spencer?"

"Nicole, please tell us in your words how the interaction at The Hilltop ended, and if there has been any communication between you and Pastor Gentry since then?" Devereux said.

Nicole pressed her hands together as if in prayer and brought them to her lips. She recalled it clearly, as if it had happened yesterday.

"He pulled his chair closer so no one could hear him," Nicole said. "Then he whispered that if he was gone, there would be a lot of hurting people in our congregation—and around the world. People who had relied on his teaching. People whose lives were a mess, who were depending on him to be there for them each week."

The men glared at her from across the table like angry wolves.

"I cried," Nicole blurted. "I couldn't handle it. He was putting this guilt trip on me. He was blackmailing me!"

"Pastor Gentry said you were distraught that morning because he told you to stop contacting him, to stop flirting with him. He said you lost it that morning. Other people saw how emotional you were."

"What they saw was me crying because he was gaslighting me! Don't you see? You have to believe me. I'm the voice calling out in the wilderness. Please, you have to believe me and take this seriously and do something about it."

"How dare you compare yourself to John the Baptist!" Landow said. "Are we done here?"

Devereux shook his head. "Let's finish this up, Nicole."

"He stood up and left me crying there. He went on the rest of the retreat as if nothing had happened."

"Have you had any contact with Pastor Gentry since then?" Devereux said.

"He texted me several times after that with the same pleas and threats. I deleted them."

"How convenient," said Connor.

"Once he heard I was coming forward, of course, he stopped contacting me."

The men were silent. Several took notes. Several just stared at her with revulsion in their eyes.

"You didn't once think maybe you should save those texts?" Connor said.

"Not until it was too late," Nicole said.

She straightened her notecards by clacking them on the table in front of her like a deck of cards. She was spent. Her stomach churned.

Devereux finished writing on his pad, leaned over, and whispered something to the attorney. The attorney spoke quietly back to him.

"Unless you have anything else to say, Nicole, we are finished."

"The last thing I'll say for the record is that Pastor Gentry is a predator. He abused me mentally and spiritually, to the point that I am not the same person I was. I struggle with depression, anxiety, and fear. Perhaps worst of all, my faith has been wounded."

The men were closing their notebooks and gathering their things to leave before she was even finished speaking.

"He ruined my marriage and family," Nicole continued, "and I am not the only one. Other women have come forward, and more will do so. It is up to you, the leaders of this church, to hear me, to hear these other women, and to respond accordingly by getting this man out of the pulpit. Fire him now, before he hurts anyone else."

"Duly noted," said Devereux. "Thank you for your time. We are adjourned."

The men stood one by one.

Conner Creed shot Nicole a nasty glare and stalked out of the room. Marshall Landow did the same.

Devereux and the attorney appeared to be waiting for Nicole to leave so they could talk.

She stood, gathered her things, then headed for the door.

Blair Post waved a hand toward the door for Nicole to leave before him.

She did and he followed closely behind her.

She walked fast down the bright hallway, her shoes clicking on the shiny white floor. She was so relieved to be done and getting out of there.

"Nicole," Blair Post called from behind.

Nicole slowed and turned to look at him.

They made eye contact, but both kept walking.

"I feel sorry for you," Blair said.

Disgusted, Nicole turned away from him and walked even faster toward the elevator, determining she would take the steps to avoid riding with him.

"You need to get professional help," Blair called. "See a psychologist."

The words hit her like sniper fire.

*That does it.*

Nicole wheeled around and marched straight for him.

She shoved his chest as hard as she could, her purse falling from her shoulder.

Blair lost his balance and staggered backward, too caught off guard to even say a word.

Nicole clenched her teeth. Her head buzzed from a rush of adrenaline. She dropped her purse all the way to the ground, jammed a foot forward, and shoved him again with every ounce of strength she could muster.

Blair flew backward, slipped on the glossy floor, and—boom—landed on his can with a loud grunt as if the air had left him.

Nicole bent down, grabbed her purse, and hurried back toward the steps, her legs feeling rubbery beneath her.

Blair yelled a string of obscenities amidst which he called her a raving psycho and promised to sue her.

*That's the least of my worries,* Nicole thought as she busted open the metal door and plunged down the steps.

# THIRTEEN

It was dusk. Darren McQue sat fuming in his car parked along the quiet street in front of Pastor Neil Gentry's large estate. The security guard at the gatehouse, a friendly older man named Lou, had remembered Darren. They caught up for a moment and Lou let Darren through. Lights were on throughout the Gentry's sprawling house, and there was movement inside.

Darren stewed.

In the past, he had stopped himself a hundred times from confronting Neil Gentry about his advances toward Nicole. He'd pleaded with God to help him forgive, to curb his anger, to help Nicole and him weather the storm.

Darren believed Nicole was telling the truth. So, to listen to those idiots from the church degrade her, treat her with sarcasm, and turn the tables on her as if she was the villain — it was insanity.

He eyed the elaborate home. The front was all stacked stone with dramatic designer lighting. The place stretched the size of a football field complete with two towering stone chimneys, a separate four-car garage, and an extra-tall wrought iron fence along back. The lawn was manicured and bordered with accent lights. Gentry had to have a maintenance crew to keep up with it all. He certainly wasn't out there doing the work himself.

*He's too important.*

Darren knew he was in a bad place, that he was off the rails, but he didn't care. The longer he sat there looking at that massive compound, the more negative he became. How did a pastor become so filthy rich? How much of the people's tithes were lining his pockets? How did he come to have a whole team of guardians from the church protecting him?

Gentry is a married man, the pastor and leader of thousands of people.

*The good shepherd.*

But really, he's a filthy, lying adulterer jet-setting around like a Hollywood star. Mr. Holiness.

*He's a home wrecker.*

Darren seethed.

He wondered how Gentry's wife Becky was dealing with all the accusations coming out against her husband. The two couples had come to know each other well over the past handful of years. They had been the closest of friends. Becky was a sweet and generous person, but she had always been fiercely protective of Neil Gentry—of his time, his schedule, his workload. She probably believed every word he said, just like everyone else.

A sense of disgust shrouded Darren.

He chastised himself for getting so sucked into Vine & Branches Church, for being played.

He'd called Dixie, their fourteen-year-old, and told her he would be later than expected. He asked her to do the bedtime routine with Dottie at 9 p.m., and to get to bed then. It was a school night.

And now, it was time to do this.

Time to confront this wolf.

*What are you going to say? What are you going to do?*

Would it come to blows?

This was a bad idea.

But Darren opened his car door anyway, got out, took a deep breath, and headed for the front door.

"DARREN!" Becky Gentry said with a tone of surprise and

hesitation after lugging open one of the the enormous double doors, made of heavy dark wood, iron, and smoked glass.

"Hey Becky, I'm here to see Neil."

Darren's voice was sober, but it cracked with emotion.

His heart hammered in anticipation.

"Oh well, darn," Becky said with a look of relief. "He's out to dinner with Ron Sawyer. You know how that goes. You don't say no to Ron."

This was not the Becky he'd come to know.

She was pretending to be nice. It wasn't genuine as it used to be.

It was no secret Ron Sawyer and his wife Jan were major donors to the church. In fact, Darren always wondered how much influence Ron had in church affairs due to the amount of money he gave.

"Where?" Darren said.

"Where what? Where they went?" Becky squinted at him and tilted her head as if to imply that was none of his business.

"Yeah—what restaurant?"

"I have no idea, Darren." Now she was getting serious.

Pastor Neil had developed a love for fine restaurants and exquisite meals.

Darren's face got hot, and he stammered. He knew he shouldn't even be there. And really—what was he going to do, go drag the pastor out of the restaurant?

"I'm sorry, Darren. I can tell him you stopped by if you want," Becky said, bouncing on her tiptoes, ready to go in. "Whatever the case, I need to get going."

The air between them was cold.

How times had changed since the two couples had been best friends.

Darren sighed.

He looked at Becky a long time, debating what to say, whether to simply turn and leave.

"You know, it was Nicole's day to give testimony today," he said.

With that, Becky's body language changed completely. She crossed her arms and twiddled her fingers against her biceps.

"Oh, was it?" she said. "I haven't been paying attention." She laughed and shook her head but was unable to hide the awkwardness. "We've had so much going on."

"Yes, it was," Darren said pointedly. "I was there. Neil's buddies were out to protect him at all costs."

*Let's see how you field that one.*

Becky's mouth sealed closed and she blinked and nodded—not saying a word.

"By 'all costs' I mean they flat out put my wife through the wringer."

Becky pursed her lips and shook her head once, as if to say Nicole deserved it.

"They are making it sound like it was all Nicole's fault, like Neil was just a poor, innocent bystander."

Becky's smile disappeared and she huffed and grasped the side of the door with both hands at shoulder height. "What is it you want to see Neil about?"

"About this. About Nicole. About his role in it."

"Fine. I'm not going to explain all that to him, but I'll tell him you came by to see him. Goodnight, Darren. Tell Dixie and Dottie I said hi."

She began to close the door.

Darren knew he shouldn't, but he stepped inside the foyer and stopped the door from closing with his foot.

It was a crazy thing to do, and he knew instantly he shouldn't have done it.

Becky looked up at him with her mouth open and her face frozen in outrage.

"You guys can't hide away in your castle forever," Darren said. "He's going to get exposed."

"Get your foot out of here." Becky kicked Darren's shin hard. It hurt, but he kept his foot where it was. She glared at him with fire in her eyes.

"You know Nicole, Becky. Do you really believe she would seduce Neil? Really? Come on, you know her better than that."

"I know my husband . . . Forget it. I'm not talking about this, Darren. You need to leave or I'm calling the police."

"Becky, come on. You're protecting him, too, just like the

elders are. He did this. He pursued a relationship with my wife. Just admit it!"

With all her might, Becky pulled the heavy door back then plunged it forward, bashing Darren's foot.

Pain shot through his toes and Darren jerked his foot away, but simply stopped the door from closing with a stiff arm.

"What are you doing, Darren? Get the heck away from my house, now!"

Darren heard one of the kids yell out to Becky from inside.

Then both kids, Eli and Hazel, came running to the door. They stopped, red-faced and out of breath, as if they'd been chasing each other around the house.

"Mr. Darren!" they both yelled with excitement.

"Hey, you guys," Darren said, breathing heavy, welcoming the reprieve.

"Are Dottie and Dixie with you?" Hazel asked, searching beyond Darren.

Becky put an arm around each child and stared at Darren with eyes full of anxiety.

"Sorry guys, they're not with me this time," Darren said.

"We haven't seen them in forever," Eli said.

"I know. I'm sorry about that," Darren said. "Maybe soon."

He started to ask how school was, but Becky wasn't having it. She told the kids to run along. They hesitated.

"Go on," Becky insisted.

Each child humbly said goodbye to Darren and headed back into the house.

Darren and Becky looked into each other's eyes and time stood still.

Their children had been the best of friends.

Their families had shared numerous wonderful times together.

Darren shook his head. "This isn't right, Becky. This is not Nicole's fault. They both had a part in it. Neil is not innocent. He thinks he can do whatever he wants."

Becky clenched her teeth and began to force the door shut again.

He couldn't read her. He wondered if she doubted her husband even the slightest bit.

"Neil's lying," Darren said. "The elders are protecting him. For the good of the church you need to—"

"You need to wake up, Darren! Your wife seduced my husband. She essentially tried to bring down our church in the process. You think God's going to let that happen? I feel sorry for you. She destroyed your family. Now, get out of here." She broke into tears.

When Darren continued to brace the door open, Becky dug her phone out of her pocket and began punching the screen. Tears shot down her cheeks. "I'm calling 911. You can hold that door open till they get here."

He took one last look at her, sighed, and disappeared into the night.

# FOURTEEN

In the dark, cool restaurant, which smelled like pine and fireplace ashes, Devina looked across the thick white linen tablecloth—which was covered with rose petals, candles, and gleaming silverware. The flickering candlelight reflected in Saul Dagon's attractive eyes as he examined the large black leather menu with the name of the restaurant embossed on front: The Oyster.

"What looks good?" she said, taking a sip from a flute of golden champagne and soaking in the ambiance.

He flicked his eyes toward her. "They have amazing scallops," Saul said. "You can't miss with any of the seafood. Fresh caught. Flown in." He sipped his champagne. "Where is she with the calamari?"

Saul spotted their waitress, a tall, thin brunette of about fifty, across the low-lit dining room, which was scattered with perhaps six other couples. He raised a hand and waved.

The waitress lifted her head, zigzagged right over to their table, and bent down to Saul.

"Calamari?" he said bluntly.

"Oh, yes sir. I'm sorry. Let me check on it."

As she scurried away, Saul mumbled something about the poor service.

In an effort to keep it positive, Devina said, "What's good

besides the seafood?" It disappointed her Saul hadn't remembered she didn't care for seafood.

He shrugged. "Lamb, duck, steak—it's all good. The chef is from Marko's in San Francisco. Best of the best."

"How do you know stuff like that?" Devina said.

He shrugged. "I read a lot. I've traveled a lot. I like nice things."

Devina smiled and nodded and pretended to read the menu.

She could never afford to come to a place like this if it weren't for Saul. She couldn't afford these clothes, shoes, perfume, purse . . . he provided all of it.

Tonight, he seemed as if his mind was someplace else. And he was agitated about something. This wasn't the first time. Once again, she wondered what was going on in Saul's world.

"Have you had a good trip?" she said. "Tell me what you did today."

As the words left her mouth, she remembered he didn't like to talk about work after hours.

"The usual," he said, swigging his champagne and rearranging his napkin in his lap. "How's everything at the condo?" Saul flipped his menu closed and leaned on both wrists over the fine table. He looked at her and, as he often did, looked past her, over her shoulder. Devina knew there was an attractive brunette behind them, seated with a man in a suit.

"Fine, fine. I love it."

His eyes returned to her. "Need anything?"

"Hmm." She contemplated for a moment. "Just that painting I want for above the couch."

"Oh, right, right," he said, glancing around the room. "I keep forgetting about that." He got his phone out and spoke into it. "Set a reminder for tomorrow morning at ten to contact Margie about artwork for Devina." He looked at her. "You gave me the measurements, right?"

She nodded and set her glass down. It was a huge space. "Five feet by five feet," she said.

"Send it to me again, will you?" he said, waving his phone. "I'll never remember."

It certainly didn't seem difficult to remember, but Devina quickly shot him a text with the measurement.

"So, how long are you in town?" she said.

At that moment, the waitress arrived with an elegant bowl of calamari, which she set in the middle of the table. He examined it briefly, then turned his hand upside down and touched the back of it to the calamari.

He looked up at her. "It doesn't feel hot."

"It just came out, sir. I've been waiting on it." The waitress's face was gaunt. Devina felt sorry for her.

"Fine." He waved her away and threw a piece of the fried squid into his mouth and fingered his napkin. He shook his head. "This didn't just come out." He pushed the bowl toward Devina and nodded at her to have some.

Her mouth sealed shut and she shook her head, mad that he'd already forgotten—or couldn't care less—that she didn't eat seafood.

She was put off by the way he'd treated the waitress. The woman probably worked two or three jobs, just trying to make ends meet.

"What were we saying?" Saul said. "Oh, I've actually got to catch a late flight tonight. Early meeting in downtown Dallas tomorrow."

*Ahh.* That was actually a relief to Devina.

"Oh, really? That's not like you—to schedule something so early," she said.

He winced and nodded, then snickered. "You know me well, my dear." He sipped his champagne. "This is a really big shareholder meeting. It's the only time we could all get together in person."

"You're an important man."

He sniffed and leaned back in his chair and looked around the room with pursed lips and an air of supremacy.

Devina glanced around the room, too, and thought about all she put up with from Saul in order to be wined and dined. If it wasn't for him, she'd be eating dollar mac and cheese in her bathrobe, watching *Wheel of Fortune.*

But was this happiness?

She felt empty.

Empty and dirty.

"Neil?" A deep male voice came from behind Devina.

Saul looked up at whoever was coming toward him and stared at the approaching person with his mouth agape, almost frozen.

"Neil Gentry?" the man said. "*The* Neil Gentry?"

Saul squinted at the man with a half-smile, then glanced at Devina, giving her a roll of his eyes as if the man was crazy.

"That is you," the man said.

Saul shook his head with question and stared up at the man, who had come from the table with the pretty brunette. He wore a dark gray suit and black tie. Clean cut. Overweight.

The large man eyed Devina, nodded at her with disregard, patted his big chest, and said, "Don Crane." Then he stood there in anticipation as if he'd just dropped a punchline and was waiting for the response.

Saul chuckled uncomfortably and shook his head slightly. "I'm sorry . . ."

"You *are* Neil Gentry, Pastor Neil Gentry . . ."

*Pastor?*

Both Devina and Saul sat back in surprise, looked at each other in confusion, and giggled.

"I'm sorry, sir. You have me confused with someone else. Have a good evening." Saul turned in toward Devina as if putting a wall up and sending the guy on his way.

The man stood there. He bent closer and examined Saul.

"Excuse us, sir," Devina said, getting annoyed.

The man stood upright, stuck his pudgy hands on his hips, and huffed. He looked over at the woman seated at his booth, then back at Saul. He patted his chest again. "Don Crane. Wheeler High School. Class of ninety-eight — same as you. I follow you on TV. Have for years. My wife loves you." He nodded toward their booth. "She didn't believe I know you. Please, will you say hello to her?"

Devina was flabbergasted. She looked at Saul, whose face was crimson. He appeared shellshocked.

"You have the wrong person," Saul said slowly, in a low voice, with finality. "Now please leave."

The short, balding maître d' arrived in his tux, straightening his thin black tie, and clearing his throat. "Excuse me, excuse me," he stepped right into the mix, speaking quietly yet sternly. "How can I be of assistance, ladies and gentlemen?"

Saul raised a hand sympathetically toward Don Crane. "This man's mistaken me for someone else. It's no problem . . . he just needs to take my word for it and leave us alone."

Saul shook out his napkin like a blanket at a picnic.

"I know this isn't your wife because I've read all about you," Don Crane blurted. "Your wife is white. Her name's Becky. I've seen all the feature stories. Is that why you're not acknowledging me, because you're on a date with a woman who's not your wife? The tabloids would love this."

Devina's mouth dropped open in shock.

Saul deflated in frustration.

"Sir," the maître d' said, "that is quite enough." He stepped right up to Don Crane and began shuffling him backward toward his booth. "Please, oblige me and return to your table and we will all be very good here. All is well . . ."

The waitress must have been watching it all because she stepped right up to Saul's table afterward to get their minds off the unpleasant affair and take their order. Saul quickly told her he wanted the Maine lobster Newburg. After catching her breath and taking another fast glance at the menu, Devina ordered the tournedos of beef with champagne sauce.

When the waitress was gone, they eyed each other and laughed with sighs of exhaustion.

"Can you believe that?" Saul said.

"My word, that was unsettling," Devina said, reaching in her bag for her phone. "He was extremely convinced."

Saul drank more of his champagne and checked his watch. He was obviously rattled.

Devina pretended to be sending a text and made a note on her phone that read: *Pastor Neil Gentry. Wife Becky. Wheeler HS 1998.*

The maître d' showed up just then, bowing at them with his hands clasped. "I apologize for that, my friends. The gentleman has left the premises. May I offer you a complimentary glass of wine or anything at all from the bar?"

"Very kind of you," Saul said. "Let's do a bottle of red, something from Spain, Tempranillo grapes, well-aged."

The maître d' nodded again. "Very well, sir," and disappeared.

"Wheeler High School's in Georgia," Devina said. "I have friends who went there."

Saul's dark eyebrows bounced; he pursed his lips. "You meet all kinds."

"Pastor!" Devina laughed. "TV! He must've had way too much to drink. His wife was so embarrassed."

Saul traced a finger around his flute, frowned, looked down, and shook his head.

Devina was surprised he wasn't enjoying the joke more with her.

"That was the oddest thing I've ever seen," she said, giddily. "I mean, he was convinced you were, what was the name? Pastor Neil somebody?"

Saul smirked and shook it off. "Yeah, I didn't catch the name."

Something about Saul's flustered reaction bothered Devina.

She tried to lighten things up by kidding, "I'm going to start calling you Pastor Saul."

Saul's mouth sealed into a slit and he shook his head. *No.*

A chill went through Devina.

Then Saul closed his eyes, shot her a sour smile, and scanned the restaurant, looking as if he was a million miles away.

The maître d' arrived showcasing a bottle of Rioja with a white linen towel draped over one arm. He went through the whole spiel of cutting the seal, uncorking the bottle, pouring a sample, and letting Saul swirl and taste. Saul seemed to welcome the distraction.

All the while, Devina was replaying Don Crane's words in her mind.

Saul appeared to be in aftershock mode.

Suddenly, Devina couldn't wait to get home and get on the Internet.

# FIFTEEN

By the time Eli and Hazel were showered and ready for bed, Becky Gentry was utterly exhausted. After Darren McQue had left, the kids had been pretty wound up, so she'd taken them to the mall before it closed to get some swimsuits and flip-flops, then to Zaxby's for a late dinner. Because Becky was hesitant to return to the house, thinking Darren might have returned, she'd even taken the kids to their favorite frozen yogurt place on the way home.

Now, Becky had just put on her light pajamas and was sitting in a chair in the master bedroom with a lamp on flipping through a magazine. She never rested well when Neil was away. She thought of him at some fine restaurant with Ron Sawyer, talking intently about budgets and capital campaigns.

Neil worked hard.

People didn't understand that.

He was working right now at 9:30 at night.

It never stopped.

The big joke in some church circles was, what does the pastor do all week? Prepare for a sermon?

*Ha. If only they knew.*

The accusations against Neil were unsettling, so unsettling.

Darren's visit was shocking. Desperate.

Her stomach turned.

Of course she had seen Neil in conversations with other women, including Nicole McQue. Sometimes laughing. Sometimes in deep discussion. But that was Neil's job. People! Relationships. Taking an interest in others. Building a church family. Setting an example of what a Spirit-filled Christian should look like.

She stopped what she was doing and stared at her dresser across the large room with its lavish furnishings and thick beige shag carpet.

*Don't look again.*

It pulled at her so badly.

Especially now that Neil had told her Nicole testified today that he had given her a necklace as a Christmas present.

She stood and crossed to the dresser.

What had Darren said?

*"Neil's buddies were out to protect him at all costs."*

She set a hand on the handle of the second drawer.

*"You guys can't hide away in your castle forever."*

She pulled the drawer open and reached into the back right side for the gray pair of Columbia socks.

*"You know Nicole . . . Do you really believe she would seduce Neil?"*

She unrolled the socks. The necklace with the small leather disc and mod silver cross dropped into her hand. Its thin silver chain had been snapped.

She stared at it for perhaps the dozenth time.

*"You're protecting him, too, just like the elders are. He did this. He pursued a relationship with my wife."*

What had this been doing in Neil's pocket?

It made her heart sick.

*Did he give this to Nicole?*

*What store did it come from? Was it bought online?*

*What if Nicole and the other women are telling the truth?*

It would be an epic scandal.

International backlash.

Becky rolled the necklace back up in the socks and placed it back where she'd gotten it. She shut the drawer and stood there with her heart pounding.

The children's lives would be ruined . . . their family would be finished.

And what about the lake house?

She debated—as she had many times—whether to confront Neil with the necklace. She'd come very close to doing so.

*What would he say?*

*How would he react?*

As things stood now, no formal legal charges had been filed against Neil. The women who had come forth with accusations against him did so to the church. Why? Because none of the women said he actually committed physical crimes against them. It wasn't sexual assault; they were calling it harassment. They were suggesting he approached them in ways that were inappropriate for a senior pastor. That would certainly be true—*if* what they were saying was true. It would then be up to the church to reprimand him, suspend him, fire him—whatever.

*That will never happen.*

Spencer Devereux, Blair Post, Connor Creed, Marshall Landow, and the other elders held Neil in highest esteem. After all, he was the reason Vine & Branches had exploded in growth and popularity. And they were in on it. They were part of the celebrity. They were on the crest of the wave, part of the inner circle—they and their wives. They were, in fact, celebrities themselves because of Neil's status.

Becky was hot. Light-headed.

She plunked to the edge of the king-size bed.

They were all caught up in it. Neil and Becky and all the insiders. They were all, in their own little way, like celebrities—at least to the thousands who attended church at Vine & Branches and followed the ministry online and on TV.

*God.*

She dropped her head into her hands.

*Is this really what you want?*

She and Neil had changed so much—the popularity had changed them, as well as the money.

*Are we pleasing you?*

They'd started out in ministry barely making ends meet. On a barebones budget. The only thing that had mattered back then was sharing God with others, bringing people closer to him. Neil had loved studying the Bible and preparing his messages. His sermons used to pierce people's hearts with the truth. And they'd been so happy. Dirt poor and brimming with joy.

She lifted her head and looked around.

Beautiful things.

Comfortable things.

Quality things.

Expensive things.

*Things, things, and more things.*

They'd become accustomed to . . . opulence.

And meanwhile, Neil's messages had changed. The focus had shifted from the truth of God's word to Pastor Neil Gentry's cleverness, his high wisdom, his funny jokes, and his showy appeal. He never used to care too much about what he wore; now, whatever city he was in, he went out of his way to shop for the finest clothes at the most luxurious stores. The only place he would get his hair cut and colored now was at Aura on Manhattan's Upper East Side.

All of it troubled Becky—if she let it.

But she didn't. She didn't let it. She wouldn't ponder such things.

She stood up and headed through the double doors of the master bedroom into the hallway, then the spacious family room with its rich, dark wood floors, designer lighting, and massive stacked stone fireplace.

A cup of hot tea . . .

She went into the white kitchen, turned on the under-cabinet lights, and put on the electric kettle.

The shrill sound of her phone startled her.

It was plugged in on the quartz countertop.

*Late for someone to be calling, unless it's Neil.*

She picked up the phone and examined the screen.

Darren McQue calling.

*What the . . .*

The gall of this guy.

"No way." She sent the call to voicemail and smacked the phone back down.

She stood there, her eyes darting about, dumbfounded that he would dare call her cell phone.

Maybe a small glass of wine would be better than tea. It'd been a long day. She went to the wine fridge.

The phone vibrated now, which meant a text message.

She crossed to it hesitantly.

Without even touching the phone she leaned over and squinted at the glowing screen. The text from Darren read:

> You're going to want to hear what I have to say.
> About where Neil is right now. Please call
> me. Now!

## SIXTEEN

Darren's heart hammered as he followed the black SUV that had picked up Pastor Neil Gentry and an attractive young woman outside the front doors of The Oyster, one of Atlanta's most exclusive eateries.

Previously, Darren had driven around the parking lots of two of Gentry's favorite restaurants in Buckhead looking for the pastor's Tesla and had decided to make The Oyster his last stop before calling it a night. He'd just happened to spot them as he was driving up a side street adjacent to the restaurant.

His phone rang over the car's speaker system.

The screen showed it was Becky Gentry calling him back. Seeing her name on the screen took him back to the times when he would see that name, or Neil's name, and take so much joy in it. Now the sight of it made his stomach twist in knots.

"Thanks for calling back," he answered.

"What is it, Darren?" Becky said, obviously annoyed. "I can't believe you're calling me. It's late."

"Five minutes ago I saw Neil leave The Oyster with a young black woman. They got into an SUV. I'm assuming it's an Uber or some kind of limo service."

There was a long pause.

Darren followed the car about fifty feet back.

"Wrong Darren," Becky blurted. "Neil drove to meet Ron Sawyer tonight. He's in his own car. You have the wrong man. Go home to the girls. Stop bothering us."

"Wait Becky!"

The line did not go dead. She was still listening.

"It's him. I don't know where his car is, but it's him. I wouldn't make this up. I wouldn't do that to you. I know it's him. And he had the young lady by the arm as they approached the SUV."

Silence at Becky's end.

"Right now I'm on Piedmont, still following them. Almost to Midtown."

"Why? Why are you doing this?" Becky said. "Even though it's not him . . . why?"

"We have to know the truth! Nicole's reputation is at stake—"

"We? Nicole? Think about Vine & Branches, Darren. Think about what this would do to all those people!"

"That's on Neil—and on you—if you know what's going on."

Again, silence.

"Nicole was one of your best friends," Darren said. "Think about what she's going through." Becky had to have doubts, especially after all the similar accusations against her superstar pastor husband.

Darren pondered where the Uber could be going—to a hotel, back to Neil's car?

"What do you plan to do—if it is him?" Becky said with a hint of yield in her voice.

Darren eyed the shiny black car as its right blinker went on.

"I don't know," Darren said. "I guess it depends where they go. I've got to get home soon."

"It's not him." She spoke in monotone.

"Do you have his phone on Find My Friends? Look. See where he is right now."

"We don't do that," she snapped.

"Of course he wouldn't want to do that. He probably goes to all kinds of places he doesn't want you to know about."

There was a click and the line went dead.

He shouldn't have said that.

He regretted it. After all, she was a victim, too.

The whole situation was a dark, sordid, ugly mess.

What was Gentry thinking, going out in public with another woman? He probably thought the restaurant was exclusive enough and far enough away from the suburbs that he wouldn't be spotted.

*Getting careless.*

Darren wished he'd gotten a photograph of the two of them, but he'd been too far away. Maybe he could still get a shot wherever they were going.

Beneath the sterile LED streetlights, traffic was busy as usual for Atlanta. Cars surrounded Darren on the congested four-lane road, and he was two cars back from the black SUV.

Nicole would have a heart attack if she knew Gentry was with another woman and Darren was following them. But Darren wasn't going to lose his focus now. He needed to be hyper vigilant following that car.

He wondered if there may still be a chance to salvage his relationship with Nicole.

That day, in the church conference room, Nicole and Darren had exchanged pleasantries. At times their eyes had met. He could see regret and embarrassment emanating from Nicole. She was remorseful. He wondered what she saw in his eyes—resentment? Sympathy? Bitterness? Doubt? Probably all of those things.

The shiny SUV turned right into the large circular drive of what looked like a high-rise condo building.

Darren followed seconds later.

The SUV pulled up underneath the porte-cochere adjacent to the gleaming gold and glass doors and stopped.

Darren pulled alongside the curb and parked about fifty feet back. The beautiful grassy circle was centered by a large, lighted fountain and surrounded by colorful azaleas and Japanese maple trees, also lit with spotlights.

Adrenaline surged almost audibly through Darren's veins as he flicked open the camera app on his phone and stared at the SUV. His hands trembled.

The black vehicle just sat there.

No doors opening yet.

*Does she live here? A call girl, perhaps?*

*Is he dropping her off or will they both go in?*

Suddenly, the back door swung open and the woman with the white high heels and tight white dress got out and headed for the entryway to the high-rise without looking back. The black SUV took off around the circle.

It all happened so fast!

There was no way Darren had time to get a photo.

Gentry would be going home to Becky.

Darren glanced at his watch.

It was too late to follow him back there, he had to get home to the kids.

But he could try to catch up with that young lady.

He turned his car off, waited several seconds for the SUV to get out of sight, and jogged up the sidewalk toward the main doors of the high-rise. As he approached, the doors slid open. A doorman in a dark suit greeted him with a nod and a smile, and asked how he could direct him.

Darren spotted the woman at a bank of elevators some thirty yards away.

"That's a friend of mine," he said to the doorman and took off toward the woman.

"Sir!" the doorman called.

The elevator doors opened. She was about to get in.

"Miss!" he yelled loudly across the atrium as he ran.

The pretty black woman's head swiveled to face him with a look of caution.

He raised a hand. "Can I talk to you one second?"

Her head craned back in suspicion. Hesitantly, she held down the elevator button, scowled, and looked around to see if he was indeed talking to her.

Darren hurried up to her, unsure what he was going to say.

"Hi. Thank you for waiting. My name's Darren McQue. My wife's Nicole." Surely she would recognize the name. Darren was out of breath, not from the run, but from the anxiety of the situation.

"Do I know you?" she said.

"No, no—but I know that man you were with." He pointed back toward the doors.

She gave a slight shake of her head and a look of annoyance. "So?"

Darren fumbled for his words. "I'm sorry. I know this looks weird but can I ask how you know him?"

Darren realized he was making a fool of himself but he didn't care.

"It's not only weird, it's none of your business. Were you following us?" she said.

Darren was instantly embarrassed.

"Is my wife's name familiar to you: Nicole McQue?"

"No. Why should it be?"

"Miss Devina?" The doorman approached in a huff from behind. "Is everything okay?"

The woman, Devina, studied Darren for a few seconds longer then looked back at the doorman. "It's okay, Sherman. I'm about to go up."

"Okay then. Let me know if you need anything. I'm right here." He walked toward the doors, glancing back several times.

"That *was* Pastor Neil Gentry in the car with you, wasn't it?" A hint of doubt arose within Darren. Could he have gotten this all wrong?

Devina's head craned back again and she squinted in bewilderment.

"Pastor of Vine & Branches Church?"

"Okay, now you're the second person tonight who's called him a pastor."

"Pastor Neil Gentry?" Darren's heart leapt. "Does he not use that name?"

Devina's posture collapsed and she mumbled something Darren couldn't make out.

"Does he not go by the name Neil Gentry?"

"Who is he to you? What's this even about?"

"He was my pastor! He seduced my wife, Nicole McQue. She's one of several women accusing him. It's all over the news."

Devina blinked in slow motion.

She shook her head as if trying to snap herself out of a daze.

Her knees seemed to buckle slightly.

Then she looked all around the quiet atrium and nodded to a bank of black leather chairs over next to a small lighted fountain. "Let's sit. Over there."

## SEVENTEEN

As DEVINA JO HAWKINS and Darren McQue sat there in the quiet lobby talking, asking each other questions, examining photos and *Washington Post* stories on their phones, and comparing notes—everything about Pastor Neil Gentry came out.

Devina was stunned.

Saul was not an oil magnate from Dallas. He was the senior pastor of a megachurch right there in Metro Atlanta.

*A pastor?*

It would have been the career she *least* expected of Saul Dagon.

The man in the restaurant earlier that night, Don Crane, had been right. Neil Gentry was indeed a graduate of Wheeler High School, married to wife Becky, father of two children, owner of a large estate—and a mansion being built on Lake Lanier.

At first, Devina insisted it couldn't be. She even showed Darren the profile for Saul Dagon on LinkedIn, and she was right, the dark photo was him, but all the information about his work and experience in the oil industry was bogus.

Fake.

*Lies.*

Darren and his wife Nicole had been close friends with Neil and Becky Gentry. Their kids had been best friends. The stories online were full of speculation and innuendo about Gentry and his suspect dealings with women from his own congregation.

Devina was just . . . blank.

*What does all this mean?*

She was apparently, possibly, one of many women.

But, really, did it even matter?

Devina knew deep down it was all a game, all temporary. Of course, that hadn't come to the surface until now. But Saul had never cared about her feelings, her hopes, her plans, her family, or background. She'd known in her heart the house of cards would collapse someday.

But did it have to end now? So soon?

Really . . . did any part of this discovery even matter? She was not some virtuous role model. She was basically an expensive call girl.

She chuckled and spoke in a daze. "He said he had a plane to catch tonight—back to Dallas. Big meeting tomorrow morning—with the shareholders."

Darren paused. "Wow."

"Yeah, wow."

"So, he never drove his own car to meet you because—"

"He was keeping up the lie he was from Texas. It's always Uber or Lyft or a limo. No wedding ring, either."

"Where did the two of you meet?" Darren asked.

Feeling comfortable talking to Darren, she explained she'd met Saul at the Publix where she'd worked, that she was from a low-income home in Stone Mountain. She was about to continue blabbing away about how Saul moved her to this high-rise and paid for everything—but she stopped abruptly.

*Keep your mouth shut. You can't be spilling everything to this guy. You've probably said too much already.*

"Well," Darren said, glancing around the fancy lobby, "you've obviously done well for yourself. What do you do now?"

She suddenly felt hot, very hot, and very threatened, and very much as if this conversation may change her entire way of life.

"Look," Devina stood. "I really need to go. This has thrown me for a loop."

Darren stood. "I understand. I can imagine. Listen, I have to ask—will you come forward, tell the church board about Gentry's false identity and—"

"Hold it, hold it, hold it." Devina put a hand to her forehead and steadied herself. "Look, I want to thank you for sharing all this information with me. Truly. And I am beyond embarrassed. I will deal with it—with him. But beyond that, no, I can't help you. I can't expose myself like that. It would ruin me. You must understand that. Now, thank you, Darren. Goodnight."

She turned and headed toward the elevators.

"Devina," Darren said bluntly. "I have to tell them."

She was afraid of that.

She stopped and turned to face him, her frustration starting to boil.

"I have to share what you've told me," Darren said, "about his LinkedIn account, how he lied to you."

"But not my name," she blurted. "You won't mention my name, or this address, where I live. I can't be brought into this."

He held up his hands innocently. "I'll try not to, but my wife's reputation is at stake. I need to prove what kind of man he is."

"Don't ruin my life, Darren. I've helped you. You've helped me. It needs to end with that. Tell them about the LinkedIn account. Tell them about how he played another stupid, gullible woman. But keep me anonymous. Please, do not bring me into this."

She clacked her high heels to the elevator and smashed the button.

Her head seemed to sway from information overload.

The lighted numbers above the doors showed the closest elevator at floor three, two, one.

"I'll try to keep you anonymous, but it's not going to be easy," Darren said from twenty feet away.

Devina stepped onto the elevator and turned around to face him. "You're a Christian, right? Do unto others?" She jabbed the button for the top floor. "I hope you live up to that."

The doors closed.

# EIGHTEEN

It was late. The Uber driver dropped Pastor Neil Gentry by his white Tesla in the Kroger parking lot on Sugarloaf Parkway. Neil cursed under his breath, annoyed how dirty his car had gotten in the few days since he'd had it detailed. He got in with a huff, hit the AC, and jumped back on I-85 headed for home. He was irritated and in a bit of a panic—which was out of character for the usually mild-mannered celebrity pastor.

The second Neil had spotted Don Crane in the restaurant that evening, he knew his charade as Saul Dagon was up. With Don's flamboyant, pushy personality, Neil realized as the big man approached that the curtain he'd hidden behind with Devina was about to be ripped wide open. She was way too smart and curious to ignore what she'd heard Crane say about Pastor Neil Gentry, Wheeler High School, his TV ministry, and his wife Becky.

Devina would get back up to her expensive condo—which Neil paid for (well, which Vine & Branches paid for)—and she would do her research.

She would find out who he was, and all of which he was being accused.

In fact, at that very moment she was probably learning everything.

To protect himself, the one thing he could do right at that moment was to delete the LinkedIn account he'd created under the name of Saul Dagon. He switched on the car's autopilot system, made sure the automobile was streaming along on its own, and called up the website on his phone. It took five minutes of scouring various pages and scrolling through fine print, but he was finally able to delete the profile.

The thing Devina would *not* learn in all the stories she was likely reading online was *his* side of the accusations. Those women, every one of them, had prompted him to act. They all had eyes for him, shining bright and lusty from out in the congregation, piercing him from across conference room tables. They all tried to bring him down. Tried to play on his human male weaknesses. Tried to destroy the empire ministry he'd built. They were all after him. Everyone wanted a piece of him and a piece of his family. Women, men, and youth—they all wanted something! It never ended.

Neil had learned. It had taken a while, but he had learned how this celebrity thing worked, and how to play the game. Sure, he'd flirted with several women in the congregation, including Nicole McQue. He was a red-blooded American man. It was fun and exhilarating and virtually impossible not to do in his position of prominence. In fact, he gave himself credit for never having crossed the line with any of them.

Devina, of course, was different. Her beauty and personality had captivated him from the first time he saw her peeking out from above a bouquet of white roses at Publix. She had become his special secret and, in a way, his saving grace. She was his outlet and shelter, the one anonymous place he could go to get away from the limelight and all of the demands of his pressure-packed career. He viewed Devina as God's way of rewarding him, meeting his needs, and keeping him sane.

Neil, who at one time had been especially fond of the Old Testament, viewed himself as a King David of sorts. Like the popular young king, many of the women had lusted after him. And paranoid King Saul and many of the men of that time were jealous of King David. And yes, King David had an affair—but God still called him a "man after his own heart."

*That's what I am.*

Neil reflected on the thousands of people who'd been saved and baptized as a direct result of his preaching and teaching.

Certainly, God was *for* Neil Gentry.

Neil truly believed he was anointed by God to bring people into relationship with their Maker.

He also believed that God not only understood his pent-up physical needs but had provided Devina as his Bathsheba. King David had, in fact, ended up marrying Bathsheba, the woman with whom he'd had an affair.

Of course, Neil knew the Bible. And he knew full well he was ignoring the fact that King David had Bathsheba's husband killed in order to be with her. He also glossed over the haunting reminder that King David suffered terribly as a result of his sin with Bathsheba—losing four of his children in the aftermath.

Neil peered out the window beneath the interstate lights, flying past neon-lit plazas and strip malls and massive corporate buildings. And he thought of his own children, Eli and Hazel, possibly dying as a result of his sins. And he buried the sick thought as quickly as it had arisen.

He was not sinning.

He was *special*.

All those baptisms—at his hands. Sometimes the success was difficult to fathom.

Surely, God would not continue growing Vine & Branches as he had if he was displeased with Pastor Neil Gentry.

Neil pictured the recent video the church creative team had produced in MTV style, showcasing his dozens of baptisms over the past year to the beat of Taylor Swift's hit, "Shake It Off."

Who else had accomplished what Neil had? He was right up there with Billy Graham, except bigger, because of the reach he enjoyed thanks to the Internet and social media.

Anyway, now the question was, what would Devina do with the information she was learning about Neil Gentry?

If she was smart, she would not say a word to Neil or anyone else. In other words, she would keep playing the game. Go on as if nothing had changed. As if Saul Dagon was indeed the oil magnate from Dallas he claimed to be. It was for her benefit! She could keep living in luxury, or . . .

*She could expose you.*
Neil's mind went blank.
He rode in silence.
He was always pleasantly awed by the quiet smoothness of the expensive electric vehicle.
*Hmm.*
A deep breath and a sigh.
*Devina, Devina, Devina.*
This was something that could not happen.
Widespread knowledge of their unique arrangement would destroy everything.
*Mmm.*
There was a man.

Neil had been introduced to him one time, briefly, by Spencer Devereux. His name was Badger, probably not his real name. Neil had been informed by Devereux on the down-low that this Badger fellow, when paid an agreeable sum, could solve any, let's say, unscrupulous problem Vine & Branches may encounter. If needed, Badger had a small team of professionals he could tap for assistance. Devereux had brought it up to Neil after *The Washington Post* ran its damning interview with that traitor, Fred Canno. But, since there was very little fallout from the story, they had let it slide.

Neil would hate to have to resort to getting an outsider like Badger involved; that would be a worst-case scenario, because it could get messy. Neil did not want messy.

Devereux was the only one who knew about Pastor Neil's friendship with Devina Jo Hawkins, and the only reason he knew was because all of her expenses had triggered red flags in the church accounting offices. Neil had explained to Devereux that Devina was a professional counselor who had become invaluable to the ministry as a sounding board and internal support system. Neil wanted access to her 24/7 and told Devereux to find a place for her services in the budget.

That was all it took; that was all it ever took.
Tell Devereux and it got done.
As he rode along quietly, Neil thought perhaps he should call

Devereux and bring him up to speed on this potentially damaging situation with Devina.

He reached for his phone and paused.

*No.*

*Why get him all worked up before it's a problem?*

*Just wait and see how Devina responds.*

If she plays it smart and says nothing, all will be well and things will continue as they are. Even if she confronted him, he would simply admit he had been forced to keep his anonymity because of who he was—a famous personality. But he would insist that his feelings for her were the same. Nothing would have to change.

Devina didn't know it, but Neil had checked her background thoroughly before getting involved with her. She'd come from an extremely poor neighborhood in Stone Mountain. Her parents had little education or money.

Harmless.

*Surely, she'll want to maintain the lifestyle we've given her.*

But she will have found out he's married—and has children.

*That could be a problem.*

Which reminded him. He popped open the compartment in the armrest, found his wedding ring, and slipped it back on his finger. Becky would notice in an instant if he wasn't wearing his wedding band. He'd come close to forgetting to put it back on several times in the past. One time he had forgotten and, luckily, she'd been asleep. He realized he didn't have it on when he was brushing his teeth that night.

God had been watching out for him.

As far as Neil knew, Devina thought he was single. He never wore his wedding ring in her presence.

Neil confessed to himself that he really didn't know Devina well enough to predict how she was going to respond to him being married. She'd mentioned once that her parents were Christians and that she grew up going to church, but the topic of her faith had never come up between them. She'd never given him the slightest impression that God was anywhere on her radar.

Silence.

Neil felt a shadow of disgrace creep over him.

He stared out the passenger window at the stores and lights and businesses shooting past. Then he looked down and fingered his gold wedding band.

The guilt he'd become so good at burying arose with sudden force.

Things with the church had happened so fast and had been so good, so rich, so high, so amazing, so remarkable—he'd lost his foundation. His faith. It was gone. Back in the dust somewhere. Behind him. Way back in the past.

Where had that young man gone who'd started out with such honorable intentions?

It had all snowballed.

As the church grew at such alarming rates, Neil's attention was commandeered by its demands.

He shook his head in astonishment, remembering those early whirlwind days when he worked nonstop from early morning when it was still dark to late at night—being pulled in a million different directions, barely having time to eat or sleep, pushing forward on sheer adrenaline.

It had all been so indescribably exciting because the kind of growth his church experienced was every pastor's dream. To accommodate all the people, Vine & Branches had moved from one building to another—bigger each time. The numbers of people who came was staggering. The church grew exponentially. Then they'd started building their own enormous buildings—all over Metro Atlanta, then in LA and Vegas and Austin, Texas. In New York City, they renovated a huge historic auditorium near Times Square and filled it to overflowing the first Sunday and every Sunday since.

Each one they built, they packed.

The money poured in.

As wonderful as it all seemed, Neil realized that's when his spiritual walk began silently dying. He had no time anymore for reading his Bible or prayer or nurturing his walk with God. Instead, every moment of the day was spent on buildings and capital campaigns and hobknobbing with major donors. And, he admitted, on shopping for the hippest clothing, investing in various businesses and properties, building the dream mansion, and searching for the latest-greatest vehicle that would bring him contentment.

Ironically, it was at that time that he'd hit superstardom, complete with feature stories in *TIME* and *People*, in *Rolling Stone*, and even on *60 Minutes*.

That kind of fame—once absorbed in a person's cells and atoms—was an addiction. The thirst for it could not be quenched.

He allowed himself to smile about his renown, about what all his high school classmates must think.

That was what was important now—that power, that fame.

As he cruised up I-85 into the night, Pastor Neil Gentry embraced the fact that he was indeed a celebrity, a successful and famous businessman devoted to the prominent empire he'd built. And he felt that empire owed him for all he'd done. *You can't feel guilty*, he told himself. After all, a number of other megachurch pastors were doing exactly what he was doing—taking a few liberties here and there with the millions of dollars that flowed in. He was glad to be friends with those other big-name pastors— some male, some female. Theirs was like a private fraternity— they were instant friends by association, sharing the worldwide limelight and distinction; and sharing some secrets of the trade as well.

For better or for worse, Becky had followed Neil's lead. And he knew he was responsible for that. She had once been a young, innocent Christian woman on fire to share her faith—pure as new fallen snow. Now, well, she'd become a product of her environment, a celebrity wife, and she played the role well. Actually, she *lived* the role, having fallen perhaps even more in love with the things of the world than he had.

The work had been grueling and had taken its toll.

They deserved to reap the benefits.

He thought of the many bridges that had burned on their way to the top, including their past friendship with Nicole and Darren McQue.

Friendly fire. Necessary losses.

*Listen to yourself.*

He didn't even study and prepare his own sermons anymore.

They paid a small team to do it. Neil had never even met them. Devereux took care of it.

Just like Devereux took care of everything, Neil had an excuse for everything. Like Devina, for example. He was helping her. Paying for everything. Treating her to nice things. Lifting her out of the gutter. Giving her a life she otherwise never would have known. Neil had trained himself to ignore the guilt and despicable nature of the whole thing, and the fact that he was a married man and a father; that she was half his age; that he was committing adultery; and that he should be leading her to Christ instead of to her bedroom.

He seethed and pounded the driver's window with the side of his fist, then slammed his head back against the headrest.

He thought of the good times they'd had with Nicole and Darren and their girls. How close they'd all been. How they'd taken so much joy in growing the church. Innocent times.

There was no going back now. Those times were history.

Neil had always had eyes for Nicole. He was a flirt. He'd allowed himself that secret enjoyment. And he'd pursued her — because he could. No one could touch him. And she was as interested in him as he was in her, no matter how she tried to make it look now.

Neil sighed as he turned off autopilot, resumed control of the Tesla, and flew off his exit ramp just a few miles from home.

Nothing was going to change. Neil knew that. He and Becky were too obsessed with their lifestyle, their cars, their homes, their possessions, and all the attention they received. They could never give all that up. They were basically trapped.

He'd taught on it at least once — on worldliness, the love of wealth. "It is easier for a camel to go through the eye of a needle than for someone who is rich to enter the kingdom of God."

In fact, those had been some of his most downloaded sermons. How did that one scripture go?

*Whoever wants to be a friend of the world makes himself an enemy of God.*

His neighborhood was coming up.

*Pull it together.*

Neil had to get his game face on for Becky — in case she was still up. Go over in his mind what he and Ron Sawyer had supposedly discussed all this time.

The feelings and sympathies and guilt and remorse he'd thought about during this ride needed to be forgotten. *"Dead to me,"* he thought, as Mr. Wonderful often said on *Shark Tank*.

Neil and Becky had enormous bills to pay.

Thousands of people were counting on them.

They needed to keep moving forward.

*No looking back.*

# NINETEEN

Curled up with her feet beneath her legs on the corner of the couch in the low-lit family room late that night, Becky Gentry tried to concentrate on the novel she'd been reading, but she couldn't read one sentence without stopping and realizing she wasn't remembering any of it.

Neil was still out. The kids had long been asleep.

He'd lied to her about where he was going that night, and she was sick to her stomach about it.

Normally, she would be in bed by now, but she had to confront her husband—about Darren's disturbing visit and follow-up call, about an unexpected call she received just minutes ago from Ron Sawyer, and possibly about the necklace—which was now snug in the pocket of the light blue pajamas she wore.

Her stomach gnawed at her from the tension and uncertainty of what was about to go down with Neil. She was almost dizzy from the prospect that the allegations against her husband could be true. She felt she and her family were on the verge of being shattered.

A big glass of wine would have helped her relax, but she wanted to be absolutely clear-headed when Neil got home. She'd determined she would wait for him no matter how late it became.

It had always nagged at her that Neil refused to link the Find My Friends app with Becky's phone. They used it for the kids' phones, so why not their own? Why couldn't they be completely open with each other about where they were, any time of day or night? With all of the rumors swirling about Neil's potentially illicit behavior, it would have been comforting to her, which should have mattered to him. But Neil was the boss. When push came to shove it was his way or the highway. It was a form of pride Becky knew well but never dared to mention.

Darren's phone call a little while ago had really upset her.

*A young black woman? Holding her by the arm? Getting into an SUV!*

There's no way it could be true. No way he would be so blatantly adulterous. And if it was true . . . then she did not know the man she'd been living with for the past twenty-plus years.

Even if Darren was wrong or lying about what he said he saw, the surprise call from Ron Sawyer a half-hour ago *proved* Neil had lied about what he was doing that evening.

In the silence of that big house, surrounded by anything she could ever want, Becky was ashamed of herself. She'd ignored the red flags. Why? Because they were now famous? Rich? Able to afford whatever they wanted, including private college, weddings, retirement, anything they wanted.

She jumped when she heard the garage door go up.

Her heart instantly began to pound.

Neil was going to be surprised that she was still up—and that she knew what she knew.

She waited there with a slight roaring in her ears as she heard the car door shut, the garage door go back down, and then—the door opening into the house.

Her heart hammered.

He was quiet because he assumed she was in bed.

"Hello," Becky called quietly, hardly able to speak. "I'm still up."

He appeared at the edge of the family room with the dark of the kitchen behind him.

"Didn't want to scare you," she said.

Neil's eyes were large with surprise. His mouth hung open. Then he seemed to snap out of his shock, smiled, sighed, and took off his dark blue suit coat. His tie was loosened and the top few buttons of his shirt were undone. He was a handsome, rugged looking man.

"What are you still doing up?" He tossed the coat over his shoulder and held it there hooked to his thumb, as if he would be off to bed in a second.

Becky stayed where she was.

"Will you sit down for a minute?" she said.

He stared at her for what seemed like twenty seconds.

She wondered if he knew he was busted.

"Sure." He tossed the jacket over a chair and made his way to the other end of the couch where he sat with a huff. "I'm wiped out."

"Darren was here," she said, realizing her body and neck were bolt-tight with tension.

"What? Darren McQue? When?"

"Not long after you left."

"What did *he* want?" Neil stood and unbuttoned the cuffs of his shirt and rolled up his sleeves and began walking toward the kitchen.

"Where're you going?" She was so nervous and had so much to say.

"Just let me pour a quick Scotch," he said. "You want anything?"

"No. He wanted to talk to you. He was very upset. He said the elders were protecting you today in their interview with Nicole."

"Of course he did," he called, followed by the sound of ice cubes clinking and alcohol pouring.

"He was defending Nicole, saying it was all your fault. It was just scary that he actually showed up here."

"He's harmless. And we've been through all that. We know they're both lying. Their marriage is imploding. He's desperate. What else is new?"

*You want to know what else is new?*

She decided to bait him along.

"Where'd you and Ron go?"

Neil came back over to the couch sipping the blond-colored drink, which he took on ice with very little water.

"Ahh. That hits the spot." He plunked down and patted her knee. "Cute PJs." He kicked off his shoes.

Her arms were crossed. She had chills from the angst of the situation. She stared at him, waiting for an answer.

"Anyway, Ron chose The Oyster. It wasn't great. Our appetizer was cold. I really don't want to talk about it, honey. Tell me what else Darren had to say. Did he come over to fight, or what was the deal?" He chuckled. "Seriously though, I've been thinking about having Spencer look into some kind of security guard for us, for each of us—"

"Ron called me." Becky dropped the bomb and examined Neil's face for the impact.

His eyes shifted—to the kitchen, to the bedroom, to his glass, and back to her. His face lit up like a bonfire. He was caught in his lie and had no words.

"He was trying to reach you with an 'urgent' question about a keynote speaker for the Horizon Conference," she said. "He called me looking for you because he had to make a split-second decision and you weren't answering your phone."

Neil was very still. He stared at his glistening drink.

*Is he thinking up another lie?*

"Where were you, Neil? Who were you with? I want the truth, right now."

He leaned forward, pulled a coaster toward him, and set the drink down.

The silence was deafening.

She had no idea what he was about to say and her entire body was numb. Her head was filled with static.

Neil leaned back on the couch and looked into her eyes.

"I'm sorry honey." He reached over and put his hand on her knee, perhaps thinking she was going to take it. *Wrong.* "I can't tell you who I was with because something is going on in the church that needs to be completely confidential. The elders told me not to tell anyone, and specifically asked me not to tell even you. It's just one of those things we can't take a chance on getting out."

He frowned and nodded and looked as if he was telling the truth.

*But what about the woman?*

Becky pulled her knee away from his hand and shifted uncomfortably.

"You lied to me." Her emotions swirled and surged.

He gave an apologetic roll of his head and moved closer to her.

But she shot to her feet.

"What else have you lied about, Neil?"

He stood and took a step toward her.

"Don't come near me. I mean it. Sit back down."

"Keep your voice down," he whispered harshly. "You'll wake the kids." He sighed loudly and sat back down.

"So if Ron hadn't called me, you would have just lived out that lie, told me you were at The Oyster with him, lied about what you two had to eat, lied about what you discussed. That's too easy, Neil."

"Now come on, honey, this is for the best interest of the church. It's all about that. We agree on that, don't we? Let's not take our sights off the prize. We've been through things like this before."

"Why didn't you just tell me the truth?" Becky stuck her fists on her hips. "Why'd you have to lie? I don't understand. Just answer." She felt tears pushing up to her eyes.

Neil sat up to the edge of the couch, leaned over, and rested his elbows on his knees. "I should have. I realize that now. I'm sorry. From now on, I'll just tell you, you know, I have a confidential meeting. You'll just have to accept that. I guess I thought this would be easier on you."

"Oh, so you did it for me." She spun around and walked away, then turned around to face him again. "This is so wrong. With all that's going on, all these allegations against you . . . how do you think I'm supposed to take this?"

She was a hair's breadth away from ripping the necklace out of her pocket and confronting him with it.

"Where were you?" she said. "Just tell me. Who were you with? Is there another woman?"

"Honey, keep your voice down, please. The meeting really was at The Oyster. Okay? That's all I can say. You're just going to have to trust me, just like with the allegations. And of course there's not another woman."

*You know what . . . I'm so sick of this.*

"Who were you with?" Becky demanded.

He shook his head. "I can't tell you that and it's nothing for you to be concerned about."

"You know what? Darren called me after he left here. He found you at The Oyster."

Neil absorbed the words and blinked as if seeing something he wasn't sure he'd seen.

Becky continued with adrenaline pumping out every word. "He said he saw you and a young black woman, arm in arm, getting into an SUV."

"That's absurd!" Neil shot to his feet and waved his arms. "He's demented. This is nothing more than the enemy trying to divide us and cause strife between us. We can't let that happen. We need to rise above that, just like we always do."

*You're using that! You use it every time!*

*I don't believe you!*

She couldn't bring herself to say those things—afraid of the fallout, afraid of ruining their marriage, possibly even afraid of him—but they screamed from within her innermost being.

She padded to the kitchen, crossed her arms, and stared out the window into the blackness trying to decide what to do next.

She heard him walking toward her.

Becky figured if she got the necklace out right then and confronted him with it, he would have an excuse for that, too. *Just like everything else.*

She needed to save it—for the right time.

She didn't want to be close to him. She turned to face him while he was still some ten feet away and announced she was going to bed.

"Okay," Neil said humbly, holding his hands up as if to calm her. "We can talk more about it in the morning, if you want."

She skirted around him and headed for the bedroom.

He did not follow.

NEIL HAD TOPPED off his Scotch and pulled the glass doors closed to the den. He sat in an oversized leather chair with his socked feet up on the matching ottoman—thinking, thinking, thinking. While he did so, he mindlessly sipped his drink and scrolled through all the new followers and comments and notifications on Instagram, which was somewhat bolstering, considering the circumstances. Sixteen new followers since last time he'd looked a little while ago: at closer examination, several of them quite attractive. Of course, he didn't follow back, he hardly ever did. The goal was to have a gazillion followers and only be following a few key celebrities, with whom he appeared to be the closest of friends.

He turned off the phone, dropped his head, sighed, and rubbed his eyes.

It was one thing to run into Don Crane at the restaurant . . . for Devina to put the puzzle pieces together and learn who "Saul" really was, which he was guessing had happened by now. That could have been smoothed over. In fact, he guessed Devina would not say a word about it. After all, she wouldn't want to give up all Saul did—and would do—for her.

But now Darren McQue had stepped into the picture.

He'd come to their home ranting and raving.

He'd apparently followed Neil and Devina earlier that night and had the nerve to call Becky and blab about it.

Becky was furious, and for good reason. But Neil felt he could contain that, too. Because, similar to Devina, Becky had grown accustomed to fine things, to getting whatever she wanted. Nice cars. The finest clothes. Anything they'd wanted for the houses. Jewelry and purses and shoes galore. And Neil believed with every fiber of his being that she would never jeopardize the lake house; that had become her baby, her passion, her obsession. Plus, Becky had become a celebrity in her own right, thanks to her association with Neil. She had her own following, which, whether she realized it yet or not, was powerfully addictive.

Reluctantly, Neil recalled the good times he and Becky had had with Darren and Nicole McQue. How close they'd been. How their families had bonded.

That was before.

It was when the church was just taking off, just starting its ascent. It had become immensely popular locally, but not nationally. It was before Pastor Neil Gentry and his wife Becky had become renowned celebrities.

There was indeed a clearcut *before* and *after*.

Neil pictured the 'before' with grainy, old-fashioned, slow-motion images in which everything was refreshingly innocent and pure and well-intentioned. Yes, the church had grown quite large, but all of their hearts and souls had been so on fire for God. His motive and sole desire back then had been to share the life-changing truths of the Bible in ways that people could apply practically in their lives.

*Boy, had it worked.*

He pictured the 'after'—the now—with high-tech color, lights, video, and flash, comical skits, loud music, fog machines, and him—appearing in the spotlight when the smoke cleared. On stage. Masses of people watching him, mesmerized, hanging on his every word.

Deep within, he knew that somewhere along the line, the focus—the product—had changed. It had shifted from God as the focal point, to Neil Gentry as the center of attention. But God was so good—he was still using Neil—in mighty ways! Bringing new people into the church every week. And God was blessing Neil and Becky beyond their wildest dreams.

Neil did not want that to change.

*Never.*

He couldn't imagine life any other way.

People loved him. They longed to even just be noticed by him. The way they all stared at him wide-eyed when he entered a room or when the lights came up on stage. The women lusted for him. The men wished they were him.

But it was in jeopardy now. Right this minute. Because of Darren McQue.

He glanced at his watch.

He'd never called Spencer Devereaux this late.

But this was urgent.

# TWENTY

Nicole McQue sat in the same chair she had the last time she'd met with Dr. Samuel Yeager. Because she'd called his direct line and said it was urgent, Dr. Yeager had agreed to meet her before his normal appointments started up that morning. It was 8 a.m. and Nicole was clutching a lukewarm cup of coffee she'd retrieved from a Keurig in the waiting room before he had ushered her into his office.

Dr. Yeager sat across from her in the same chair as last time, dressed crisply, professionally, and smelling nicely with a hint of expensive cologne. He listened intently as Nicole opened up about Pastor Neil Gentry's advances toward her and about her questioning at the church the previous day. She admitted her mistake of having had feelings for Gentry. She told him about the necklace, about how she had insisted the relationship end, and about how Gentry threatened to take his own life if they couldn't be together.

"The elders yesterday," Nicole fought back tears, "they just completely tore me down. They insinuated this was all my fault. They said I was being dramatic. They implied I was the one making advances toward him, trying to make national headlines. They basically said I need mental help. It's . . . it's unbelievable. If people knew what was going on . . ."

Dr. Yeager asked Nicole how the meeting ended the day

before and Nicole—with a blubbering mixture of laughter and tears—told him how she shoved Blair Post to the floor and stalked out of there. Dr. Yeager gave a hint of a smile.

"I needed to talk to someone, to you. I felt like I was going to have a nervous breakdown," Nicole said. "Thank you for seeing me on such short notice."

"I'm glad you called," Dr. Yeager said. "Unfortunately, we are hearing more and more about how some megachurches are copying celebrity culture. They're being built around these personalities—people who end up having immense power. Before you know it, you've got an abusive culture and a controlling form of leadership."

"That's exactly what it is. Exactly."

"It sounds to me like this pastor got to you, emotionally. He showed interest in you—which had to be flooring, coming from someone as famous as he—and you opened up to him. And now, because you've come out against him, he's using some of the feelings you had for him as ammunition against you."

"Correct," Nicole said, "and it makes me look like an absolute fool. And the thing is, as mad as I am at Neil Gentry, I'm even madder at the church leaders who I loved and respected and served with. They don't believe me, and they failed to protect me. And now they're trying to throw me under the bus in order to protect their leader."

Dr. Yeager nodded. "It is going to hurt for a while, Nicole. The church is supposed to be a safe place. This isn't supposed to happen there. It is so wrong on so many levels." He removed his black glasses, held them in his lap, and looked at her. "You've been betrayed by an entity that is supposed to be a source of hope and strength and security. Instead of safety and shelter, the church for you has become a place of hurt and betrayal and fear. This is more common than you might think."

Nicole cried openly because of the relief she felt in opening up and talking about it. Because a wise, sober, honest man—a doctor, a professional—believed her and sympathized with her. He was affirming what she'd been thinking and it made her feel sane when she'd been questioning her sanity.

He handed her the trusty box of tissues. "Vine & Branches has been in the news a lot lately," he continued. "It seems to have a consistent narrative of perception management and cover-up. What you're experiencing, Nicole, is quite possibly a form of spiritual abuse, a form of emotional and psychological abuse. From what you've told me, and what I've read, Vine & Branches may be demonstrating a systematic pattern of coercive and controlling behavior—in a religious context. And that hurts people. It leaves a deeply damaging impact on those who experience it. But I'm hopeful you can work through this. Just being here today is progress."

Nicole's head dropped to her chest. She squeezed her hands and fingers. She took a giant breath and blew out through her mouth slowly. She was trembling.

"I miss my girls," she said.

He asked her when she had last seen them.

She explained and then added, "I was surprised Darren showed up for the meeting yesterday. He tried to stand up for me. He was furious about how the elders were shielding Gentry."

"That's a good sign. Very positive."

"I don't know if he'll be able to forgive me. I mean, I did succumb to Gentry's advances. I was weak and I let myself have feelings for another man. What if Darren and I try to get back together and he realizes he can never trust me again? That scenario keeps playing over and over again in my mind. Like I've ruined things for good and there's no going back."

"We can work through that together. Eventually, I can meet with him one-on-one, then with both of you. It's going to be one step at a time. But I like your mindset. You seem good today."

"Lots of emotions," she blurted and cried and broke into more tears.

He nodded sympathetically.

"It's good to be able to share what you're feeling. And what you're feeling is all perfectly normal."

Nicole's watch vibrated. She looked at it.

*Odd.*

It was a call from Sheryl Ferguson. In Nicole's absence, Sheryl and Darren took turns carpooling her kids and their kids to school, and it was a few minutes past pickup time.

"I'm getting a call I've got to take—about my kids," Nicole said as she fished in her purse for her phone. She found it, stood, excused herself, and answered the call as she walked over to the window.

"Hey Nicole, it's Sheryl Ferguson. I'm sorry to bother you. I normally wouldn't call you—"

*Yeah, that's because I'm the black sheep . . . it's as if I have leprosy.*

"Hi Sheryl," Nicole said a bit on edge. "What's going on?"

"Darren hasn't shown up for Wells and Robby yet."

The words registered hard and Nicole put her hand on the windowsill to steady herself.

"He's usually right on time. He's never late," Sheryl said. "I've tried to call him but he's not answering. I thought you might know . . ."

Her words faded out. Things slowed down. Slowed way down.

*Dixie and Dottie.*

"Nicole? Are you there?"

"I'm not sure what's going on, Sheryl. You're right, he's never late. Why don't you go ahead and take Wells and Robby to school. I'll find out what's going on. Hopefully we'll be back on schedule tomorrow."

Nicole ended the call, scrolled, and called Darren.

"I'm sorry," she said to Dr. Yeager. "Mix-up with carpool."

Dr Yeager stood. "It's okay. We can be finished. I really need to get going anyway."

Nicole nodded, needing to get somewhere private.

Dr. Yeager gave a wave and Nicole darted out of the office, through the reception room, and out into the shiny white, sterile hallway.

Darren's phone went to voicemail.

As she paced and waited to leave a message, her phone vibrated.

It was Dixie calling.

Nicole's pulse pounded. She focused hard on which button to choose. Her hands trembled violently. She fumbled the phone, dropped it, but snatched it on its way to the floor. She focused again and pressed the button that ended the call with Darren and accepted the call from Dixie.

"Hello, Dixie?"

"Mom, Dad's not here."

"What do you mean he's—"

"We overslept. We don't think he came home last night."

## TWENTY-ONE

Devina had awoken that morning to the sound of her cell phone alerting her to a text message from Saul, who she now knew to be the megachurch pastor, Neil Gentry.

> Good morning sunshine. Made it back to Dallas. Heads up. A guy will be there to hang your artwork this morning. He'll text you when he gets there. You're welcome.

As the coffee pot gurgled and Devina dashed around in her robe and slippers moving the couch and end tables and lamps to make room for the installer, she wondered how Saul had arranged for someone to pick up that huge painting from the gallery this early—*and* install it.

Perhaps he cared more about her than she realized.

She'd slept longer than usual because she'd stayed up past midnight watching YouTube videos of the popular pastor and reading news stories and feature articles about Neil Gentry's past, his marriage and family, his mega-popular ministry, his growing fortune, and his alleged trysts with women from his own congregation.

It was all dizzying.

*Darren McQue hadn't been lying.*

Devina could only hope he would keep her name out of the headlines.

As she scooted things around with the morning sunlight streaming into her condo, a bittersweet feeling came over her, reminding her that she had this spacious, modern place to call home—her very own home—thanks solely to the deceiver she'd learned about the night before.

Was he really in Dallas? Probably not. The stories said he lived in a suburb of Atlanta. She knew that now. And, like the sun coming up, it was dawning on her that Saul Dagon was probably a pathological liar.

Everything was up in the air now and Devina realized she had some major decisions to make.

As she bustled about, wondering if she would have time to shower before the installer arrived, her mind was consumed by all she'd learned about Saul—Neil Gentry. Did his wife Becky have any idea he was cheating on her, that he had a live-in "call girl" right there in Atlanta? Devina was ashamed to think of herself in such a way. Becky couldn't know! She would never stay with him. Devina had watched clips of interviews with her and she'd seemed so clean and wholesome, so professional, and above reproach.

What about the other women? Had Neil slept with them as well? It was unfathomable, because his sermons—the bits and pieces she had listened to online the night before—had made him come across as so . . . righteous. So upstanding. As if he was an authority on Christianity.

He was truly convincing.

And so charismatic.

The people in the audiences were literally leaning into every word he spoke. They all had their Bibles and notebooks and scribbled like fiends.

She wondered if her parents knew of Pastor Neil Gentry. They were conservative Christians. They always had the TV tuned into those religious channels. It was feasible they even admired the man who was sleeping with their daughter.

Devina went to the kitchen and poured a cup of coffee. She crossed to the sliding doors, opened one, and stepped outside into the sunshine. She needed a few seconds to get her head together. She sat in one of the patio chairs overlooking the rooftop swimming pool, sipped the coffee, and closed her eyes.

She was 95 percent sure Neil Gentry didn't love her. And she was quite certain she didn't love him. It was an arrangement. No more, no less.

With the quiet came the realization that the keg of dynamite she was sitting on may lead to a pot of gold. Neil Gentry was known around the world. And she was his . . . mistress. Women wrote books about stuff like that, or they sold their stories to magazines like *National Enquirer*—for lots of money.

Honestly, though, Devina would be content going on just as things were. She had everything she wanted. She didn't have to let on to Saul that she knew anything about who he really was.

She looked around at the crystal-clear pool and the fine landscaping and the surrounding skyscrapers. Several workers were trimming hedges, and one was sweeping the pool deck.

Darren McQue was going to expose Pastor Neil Gentry—very soon. Would he keep Devina's name out of it?

*How can he?*

Surely, people will find out who she is, where she lives . . .

Her phone buzzed in the pocket of her robe, startling her.

She checked it.

A text message.

> Hi Miss Hawkins. I'm here to install your artwork.

Devina thought for a second then took her coffee inside and slid the door closed.

She went over and checked herself in the mirror.

The light pajamas and robe were too flimsy.

She texted him back.

> Give me five minutes then text me back and I'll be ready for you.

She dashed into her spacious bedroom, entered the marble

bathroom, brushed her teeth, splashed hot water on her face, dried off, and rolled on some deodorant.

She was so excited to see the large painting she'd had her eye on for so long. It was a square abstract with brilliant oranges, blues, and yellows. Surely the installer must have help. He couldn't get that up here by himself. In the huge walk-in closet she quickly disrobed and threw on sweatpants, a bra, and a sweatshirt. Next, she sat on the leather ottoman, leaned over, and put on black anklet socks and her favorite yellow Hokas.

She looked at the time and headed back to the kitchen to pour more coffee.

Her phone buzzed and she checked the text message.

> Hi it's the installer again. Are you ready for me now?

"Me?" Somehow, he was doing it himself?

Instead of coffee, she headed for the little security keypad at the front door and texted him back.

> Yes. Where are you?

He texted right back.

> In the lobby.

She responded.

> Come on up. Do you know where my unit is? Top floor.

He texted back:

> Yes, I know.

*Hmm. Saul had told him everything. Very good.*
She texted him back:

> Let me know if you have any problem.

He texted her back a thumbs up.

She went back in the living room and re-checked the space she'd left him on the wall where the painting would hang. She got behind the couch and shoved it out another foot. There was plenty of space for him to work and if he needed more, he could move things himself.

Devina returned to the coffee maker and poured another cup.

She stood there at the island holding the cup in both hands, thinking about what she was going to do that day. She needed a few things at the grocery, and there were two lamps at Pottery Barn she wanted to look at again now that the painting would finally be up.

For the time being, she would continue communicating with Saul as if nothing had happened.

She wondered if she would hear any more from Darren McQue.

She hoped not.

Her phone buzzed. It was a text from the installer.

> I'm here.

Then there was a weak knock at the door.

Devina excitedly breezed through the sunny living room, imagining the painting on the wall, and swung the front door open. "Hello—"

The man wore black from head to toe, including a black ski cap.

His black-booted foot stepped inside the doorway and planted there.

His dark eyes met hers.

His face was void of expression and rough with black and gray beard stubble.

Devina looked all around him for the painting. She scanned the hallway.

There was no painting. No helper.

Her mouth fell open.

He lifted a black gloved index finger to his lips. "Shhh."

His eyes were sad and dead.

He lifted the other gloved hand, pointed, and said, "Go inside."

# TWENTY-TWO

Nicole McQue's first instinct when she heard Darren hadn't come home the night before was to get to the house, to the girls—which she did in record time.

The whole way to the house, she had envisioned Dixie and Dottie in a frantic state, waiting at the front door, watching for her on pins and needles.

Not so.

*Not even close.*

Instead, the sisters had prepared waffles and fruit for breakfast, made their beds, and were dressed for school, which, unbelievably enough, started the first week of August in Atlanta. They'd been back in classes for several weeks.

It was odd stepping back into their world—the house, the routine. The place was clean and organized. She expected nothing less with Darren in charge.

Nicole tried her best to play along with the girls that it was no big deal Dad hadn't returned home the night before, even though she knew Darren would never do such a thing unless he was in dire straits—unless something was very wrong.

As Nicole expected, the girls were slightly crabby toward her —Dixie especially, being the older one, the one who probably understood more clearly that her mother had done something dishonorable. They hadn't seen each other in about a week. And when the younger Dottie saw Dixie giving her mother the cold shoulder, Dottie remembered she was supposed to do the same, and followed suit. For better or worse, they were developing tough skin at an early age.


SINCE THE GIRLS were ready and wanted to go to school, Nicole decided to play along with it and drive them. It would probably be best having them away when the police came. As the girls headed for the car, Nicole checked all around the downstairs to see if there was any sign that Darren had possibly come and gone, but there was no trace.

Once she'd dropped the girls at the school office, sending them both in with hand-written notes stating that it was her fault they were late, she immediately got on the phone with the police to report Darren's disappearance.

Unlike in the movies where they say a person needs to be missing a certain amount of time before a report can be taken, the investigator she was finally forwarded to, Detective Scottie Benson, said he would take the report personally and agreed to meet Nicole at the house when he could get free that morning.

In the meantime, Nicole tried Darren's phone again and was sent to voicemail. His Find My Friends app wasn't working either because he'd turned it off when they had separated.

Back at the house, Nicole put hot water on to boil and paced the kitchen, running through all the possibilities of what could have happened to Darren. Did he run his car off the road? Was he in an accident and she hadn't been notified yet? She could call the local hospitals. Where had he gone yesterday when he was forced to leave her questioning at the church.

As she poured her tea she fell into a dreamlike state, standing there staring at the teabag steeping, wondering if the unthinkable could have happened. Could Pastor Neil Gentry or Spencer Devereaux or the elders have had anything to do with Darren's disappearance?

Chills ran down her arms.

*They wouldn't do that. They would never go that far.*

It was an insane thought, but . . . the whole mess had been

inconceivable. The way the church leaders were covering up for Neil Gentry was scandalous. It felt to Nicole as if there were dark, unseen forces at work that were stacked against them, like a corrupt corporate giant was steamrolling them, crushing them from an untouchable high castle.

The sound of the doorbell made Nicole jump.

*Detective Scottie Benson.*

She took in a deep breath, exhaled slowly, and took a drink of the tea.

*God, let this man find Darren.*

On the way to the door, it dawned on her that she should have the detective check the footage from the front security camera to see if there had been any sign of Darren—or anyone else—coming or going through the night. After several neighborhood break-ins, Darren had put up small security cameras on the front and back of the house.

Nicole got to the door and glanced out the narrow vertical window on the side.

It was not Detective Scottie Benson standing there, as she'd presumed.

She froze.

Her stomach turned with a sour uneasiness.

It was the last person she would ever expect to see at her home.

Nicole's heart raced and she contemplated sneaking back into the house, pretending not to be there. But her car was out front—

"I see you, Nicole," the familiar female voice called from outside. "Please . . . open up."

~

STANDING outside Nicole and Darren McQue's front door that sunny morning, Becky Gentry was nervous and fearful about what she was about to find out about her husband—the man who was looked up to by thousands of people around the world. The man who seemed to be keeping damaging secrets.

After Becky's confrontation with Neil the night before, she had barely slept, partly because Neil had never come to bed. It turned out he'd slept in one of the guest rooms and left the house early that morning.

Wide awake in the night, Becky had the strongest premonition that she needed to take the necklace to Nicole and ask her about it face-to-face, just the two of them. It had to be done, even though Becky was apprehensive about what would be revealed. She had to know the truth.

After ringing the doorbell and waiting, Becky saw movement in the foyer and and it appeared Nicole might pretend she wasn't home. Becky called out for Nicole to please open up. The two women hadn't seen each other in months due to the accusations swirling in the Vine & Branches community.

Finally, the door nudged open slightly. Nicole stood there on the inside, saying nothing, just staring at Becky with tired eyes and many creases Becky had never seen before.

"I tried your apartment first," Becky said. "Can I come in?"

When Nicole didn't move, Becky said, "I won't stay long. I promise."

"What's it about?" Nicole said flatly. "Is it about Darren?"

Becky stopped in her tracks, recalling Darren's visit and calls the night before. "No . . . It's about something that's been bothering me, something that only you can help with."

Nicole's eyes closed slowly, her mouth sealed shut. She frowned. Then the door opened slowly.

Becky stepped inside and turned to pull the door closed.

"Darren didn't come home last night," Nicole said. "You don't know anything about that, do you?"

Becky froze for a second, dumfounded, her mind racing through the previous night's events with Darren. She turned from the closed door to face Nicole. "No. My word, Nicole, I'm sorry. What happened?"

Nicole was only wearing light makeup. Her hair was frizzy. Her cheeks appeared hollowed; she'd lost weight and looked gaunt.

"Don't know," Nicole said. "Police are coming to do a missing person's report. Let's make this quick."

Becky felt she had no choice but to tell Nicole what had

happened the night before. "Darren came to our house last night," she said.

Nicole's eyes bulged. Her mouth dropped open. "What for?"

Becky shook her head, trying to decide what to say and what not to say. "He was looking for Neil." Becky recalled with a sick feeling Neil's lie about who he'd been with. "Neil wasn't home. Darren was upset. Really upset. He was going on and on about how the elders took Neil's side at your testimony."

"That's it?"

"Basically, yeah."

"Did he say where he was going because, again, he didn't come home all night. The girls were here alone. He wouldn't do that. Something's wrong."

Becky's stomach churned and a terrible feeling came over her. This whole thing was becoming severely disturbing.

"Darren was trying to find Neil," Becky said. "He called me later and said he had found him—at The Oyster."

"What?" Nicole blurted. "Why? Why would he follow him?"

"I told you—he was mad. He wanted to have it out with Neil, I guess. I don't know."

Nicole sighed loudly and crossed her arms. "What else happened. I need to know everything—to tell the police."

Becky paused, took a deep breath, and did what she had to do. "Darren texted me later and said he'd found Neil. He said I would want to know where he was, and who he was with," Becky said, embarrassed and wondering what damage would come of this testimony. "He wanted me to call him."

Nicole's face morphed into a look of utter shock. She appeared to be unable to speak.

Becky was trapped. She had to tell Nicole what Darren had said, because Darren was missing. It was the right thing to do, even if it leaked out and implicated Neil in a negative light.

*Where could Darren be?*

In a thought that left her as quickly as it had come, Becky wondered if Neil or the elders could possibly have had anything to do with Darren's disappearance.

"Did you—call him?" Nicole asked with bated breath, as if teetering on the edge of a cliff.

"I did. Darren said he was parked outside The Oyster. He said he saw Neil get into an SUV with a young black woman."

Nicole's hands shot to her face in the prayer position. Her eyes darted back and forth in confusion.

"I asked Neil about it when he got home last night." Becky would not divulge to Nicole that Neil had lied to her about being with Ron Sawyer. "He said he was out on a confidential church matter—"

"Oh, come on Becky—wake up! When are you going to face the truth? How many women need to come forward? How many lies has he got to tell before you call him out on it?"

Now Becky was the one who was speechless, feeling a glimmer of truth in Nicole's bold words.

"Forget it," Nicole spat. "I'm not getting into that now. Did Darren confront Neil? Did they get into a fight or something?"

Becky threw up her hands, trying to recall her conversation with Darren, and then with Neil. "No . . . I don't think so. I mean, Darren just told me what he saw. And Neil did not mention seeing Darren. I'm pretty sure he didn't or he would have told me."

"Oh, sure he would, because he's so honest with you," Nicole said sarcastically. "So the last you knew, Darren was at The Oyster."

"No, no . . . He followed them from there. He said they were on Piedmont, almost to Midtown."

"Then what?"

"I asked him what he planned to do and he said he didn't know. That's the last I heard from him. But, again, when Neil got home and I told him about talking to Darren, he acted as if he had no idea Darren had followed him."

"Where's Neil now?"

"Probably at the church. He left early this morning."

Nicole wrung her hands and stood there deep in thought.

Becky dropped her head, trying to decide if she should just leave. She'd already made the mistake of giving Nicole ammunition that could be used against Neil; but she'd had no choice about that. The police were about to be involved. If she got out the necklace in her pocket and Nicole said it was indeed the one Neil had given her as a Christmas present, Nicole would have that against them as well. But, in the night, Becky had decided if that happened she would vehemently deny she was ever even at Nicole's home.

Becky just needed to know the answer but, grimly, she was almost sure she already knew.

"What is it you want, Becky? I've really got to get going. This investigator should be here any minute."

Becky shook her head. "Forget it." She walked toward the door. "I'll ask you another time. Darren comes first right now. I hope he turns up soon."

Becky opened the front door, thinking not another word would be spoken.

"Becky," Nicole called as she followed her to the door.

Becky turned around to face her. They were just four feet apart.

"Why would I lie about any of this? We were best friends."

Her directness staggered Becky, like a punch to the jaw. It was obvious that, with Darren missing, Nicole felt she had nothing to lose.

"Neil pursued me. He initiated it—"

Becky's anger flared and she began to object.

"Just let me finish," Nicole said. "I admit, I fell for it. I'm to blame, too. And I'm forever sorry about my weakness. I'll pay for it the rest of my life. I may lose my marriage and kids over it. But my gosh, Becky, Neil is a player. He's a manipulator. He's a controller. And he's a liar. He should not be the head of that church. That's the last thing he should be."

Becky felt as if she was against the ropes in a boxing ring, taking shot after shot to the head and body. She found herself gripping the doorframe with one hand to remain balanced; her other hand was stuck to her forehead. She was unable to speak. Rage and defensiveness and pride arose within her, but Nicole's words just kept landing, one after another. And Becky knew Nicole, knew her to be a good person. And somewhere deep, deep inside, Becky knew every word was true.

It hurt. It hurt so badly.

It also threatened everything Becky and Neil had—the wealth, the prominence.

Nicole said, "Now I'm going to tell you something and you can ask Neil about it—or you can bury your head in the sand."

Becky could only stare at Nicole with her mouth agape.

"You ask Neil what he had to say about *you*. About your out-of-control spending. About you wanting to have an equal amount of the limelight. About you being so attached to the houses and cars and clothes that nothing anyone could do could release your grip on those things. Not even his relationship with me."

Becky stared at Nicole blearily through eyes brimming with tears. Her heart was crushed. Her hopes were dashed. She felt as if she were standing in dust and ashes.

"I hate to tell you these things. I hated to hear them. It was pure evil. But something's got to *register* with you, Becky. Something's got to *jolt you* out of your slumber."

Becky's tears spilled down her cheeks and she staggered backward.

Nicole grabbed her arm to steady her.

Becky broke out crying, yanked her arm away, turned and ran for her car.

# TWENTY-THREE

Pastor Neil Gentry leaned the soft beige leather seat back on the Gulfstream and lifted the window shade. He kicked his loafers off and rubbed his feet on the thick carpet of the plush jet cabin. Outside, the morning's golden sun silhouetted other small planes on the tarmac at Peachtree DeKalb Airport, also known as PDK, a small but busy air strip near the Atlanta suburbs of Chamblee and Brookhaven.

The curtain up front parted and Sienna, a tall woman of about thirty with long straight blond hair and high heels, smiled at Neil and approached carrying several napkins and a flute of mimosa. She wore a navy skirt, matching jacket, and a starched white shirt. She set the tall glass on the wide polished wood armrest with built-in coasters.

She leaned near him, smelling like lilacs, as usual.

"Can I refresh your coffee, Pastor Gentry?"

Neil shook his head with a frown. "You can take it."

She reached over and removed the sleek, gold-rimmed coffee cup as he took his first sip of the mimosa.

"Whoa, whoa." He lifted the glass to her. "More champagne. A lot more."

*You'd think she'd remember that.*

Sienna nodded with a smile and headed for the kitchen.

"Sienna," Neil called.

She turned back.

"Turn up the AC, please. It's stuffy in here."

She gave a slight nod and smile and disappeared behind the curtain.

In the distance outside, finally, he spotted the expected black limo, gliding toward the Gulfstream as smooth as a sled on snow, coasting in like something out of a movie.

Neil's life seemed like a movie.

The fame.

It was all so surreal.

But pastors were not supposed to be famous. Or rich.

There was something wrong with this picture. *Very wrong*. He'd known it for a long time. But . . . he was on autopilot. The trajectory was locked in. He wasn't going to change. It was all too good.

The limo came to a stop next to Neil's jet and he heard and felt the bump of the Gulfstream's staircase folding down toward the tarmac.

Neil continued watching as one of the back doors of the limo opened and the trunk popped up.

Badger, a rough looking man wearing all black got out, surveyed the grounds, and quickly walked around the back of the limo. He opened the back passenger door and said something.

Devina got out, stretched her shoulders back, and turned to look up at the windows of the Gulfstream.

Neil slowly leaned back to avoid eye contact.

This would be their first meeting since she knew who he really was.

The man in black hoisted her big suitcase out of the trunk, rolled it up next to her, and then they both made their way to the stairs of the jet. Devina wore a faded denim jacket over a soft, olive-green dress. Also wearing a straw Panama hat and casual strappy sandals, she looked as if she was going on vacation.

Sienna produced the re-made mimosa and waited for his approval.

Neil sipped it, nodded, and waved her away, grateful the drink was now almost all champagne.

He needed it.

He took a second to get in the proper mindset for Devina.

He settled back in his seat and put his feet up on the high-gloss coffee table, made of reclaimed eastern hemlock.

*Important to appear relaxed and in charge.*

Voices came from the front of the small jet.

Neil ran his fingers through his hair, brushed off his shirt, cleaned his teeth with his tongue, and took a long swig of the mimosa.

The man in black known as Badger popped his head in first.

"Pastor Gentry?" he said.

Neil nodded and waved him back.

Badger ducked back out, the curtain opened fully, and Devina came through first. She stopped fifteen feet away when she saw Neil and gave him a blank stare. Then her eyebrows jumped and she headed toward Neil with a big black leather bag over her shoulder.

Badger followed her, removing his black ski cap and stuffing it in his back pocket. He had on black pants and boots, and a black track jacket. He wasn't a big man, but he looked tough, not an ounce of fat on his rigid body. About fifty years old. His face was weathered and his eyes were like steel.

"Her suitcase?" Neil said.

"They're putting it in cargo load," Badger said.

"Very good, Badger," Neil said. He looked at Devina and said, "Give us a second, will you, dear?"

"Certainly, *Pastor*." Devina said the word with disgust, turned, walked back, entered the lavatory, and locked the door.

Neil ignored it, for now.

"Good to see you again." Neil raised his hand and shook with the man in black.

"Yes, sir. Good to be here."

"Any problems with this today?"

He shook his head concisely, one time. "No, sir. All very amicable."

Badger gave an awful, phlegmy cough in the elbow of his jacket and said, "Excuse me, sir."

Neil gave a sniff but didn't smell anything Badger may have been smoking.

"And the condo?" Gentry said.

"All being taken care of as we speak, sir."

"What about her phone?"

"Left it in the condo for the cleaners, as instructed."

"Good. Listen, I know I told Devereux we wouldn't need you to make this trip," Neil said, "but I've changed my mind."

Badger gave a nod. "Certainly, sir."

"I don't want you on this flight," Neil said. "Plus you'll need to get some things together. Just pack for a day or two. Get the first flight you can today. Meet us in Vegas at the MVR."

Badger's head tilted and he squinted. "MVR, sir?"

"Oh, sorry," Neil said. "Mission Valley Resort. It's our meditation ranch just outside Vegas. In fact, have Devereux's people book the flight for you and arrange for your ground transport. It'll be much faster that way."

Badger clasped his thick hands in front of him and nodded. "Very good, sir."

## TWENTY-FOUR

DEVINA SAT on the closed lid of the glossy wood toilet in the tiny lavatory of the Gulfstream, calculating how much danger she was in. The man in black—Saul had called him Badger—had forced his way into her condo, taken her phone, and told her to get dressed and pack for a three- to five-day trip. The man had never produced a gun or weapon and had not threatened her, but he didn't have to—Devina knew he meant business. He had a confident air about him that was quiet yet forceful. He'd simply told her she would be the guest of Saul Dagon. "You mean Pastor Neil Gentry," she had responded. When Badger said nothing in response, she'd asked him where they were going so she could pack accordingly. Badger responded in almost a whisper, "Las Vegas. Make it quick."

Devina could not fathom that Saul—Neil Gentry—would hurt her.

She suspected her conversation the night before with Darren McQue had to have had something to do with her present circumstances.

Or maybe it was the run-in at the restaurant with that man, Don Crane, Saul's high school classmate. Saul must have known Devina's curiosity would be piqued and she would go home, do her research, and find out who he really was.

The brief knock at the lavatory door startled her.

A muffled female voice said, "Pastor Gentry is ready for you." It was the flight attendant, the tall blond.

Devina said nothing. She stood and checked herself in the mirror. She took the hat off, fidgeted with her hair, placed the hat back on, took a giant breath, exhaled long and slow, and opened the door.

The curtain up front was closing and Saul was alone in the cabin.

He motioned for her to sit across from him. Then he pointed to a mimosa that had been poured for her and was sitting in the coaster next to her seat.

"Did Badger take good care of you?" Saul sipped his drink.

Devina plopped down with a huff. "You've got a heck of a lot of explaining to do. Why'd you lie about the artwork? Why didn't you just ask me if I wanted to go to Vegas instead of having some thug haul me over here? What's this about, *Saul?*"

Gentry closed his eyes and interlocked his fingers in front of his face. "You know who I am now."

"Yeah, I do. So, it's all been a lie."

"Not really. I'm the same person you've known all along."

"Yeah, only your name, your job, and your home are lies. That's all."

"I have no one else like you, Devina—"

"Except your wife. I think her name is Becky. Oh, and your kids, let's not forget about them."

That seemed to sting him. He turned and looked out his window.

"What are we doing? Why Vegas? Why now?" she said. "What's this about?"

"I couldn't tell you who I really am." He continued staring out the window.

"The reasons are obvious."

"Yeah, because you're supposed to be a man of the cloth. Ha." She shook her head. "If your millions of followers only knew . . ."

He turned back to face her with a solemn look on his tan face. "I don't want to lose you. I *can't* lose you. You're what holds me together."

The words touched her. And that was ridiculous because their relationship had been built on nothing but lies and lust and gifts and scandal. But he'd never been serious with her like this. He'd never shown much of any genuine affection toward her.

"Can you keep it between us?" He reached over and covered her hand in his. "It's vital that you do—"

"I looked up Saul and Dagon in the Bible last night. Why that name?"

He shrugged. "I have no idea. Pulled it out of thin air."

"Dagon was a god in the Old Testament. They built a temple for him," Devina said.

Gentry nodded with a frown and blinked slowly. "First Samuel."

"They brought the ark of God into Dagon's temple and sat it next his statue. The next morning Dagon was flat on his face. They set him up and the next morning the same thing happened, but Dagon's arms and legs were broken off."

Gentry threw up his hands and gave a look like he didn't care. "I have no idea. I must've been studying that when I met you."

"And Saul. He sure didn't turn out to be a very good king," she said. "He was proud—and paranoid."

Gentry's teeth clenched, as if he was swallowing back a sea of emotion.

Finally, he spoke. "Can you keep this between us, or not? That's what this comes down to. Bottom line."

"What if I don't?"

He shrugged. "Then we part ways." He threw his head back and drained his glass.

"Just like that?"

He nodded. "But I don't want it to be like that." He moved closer to her. "It doesn't have to be. Listen to me."

"So, you're saying if I want it to end, it just ends. We part ways. No hard feelings."

He stared at her for a long time. "Correct."

"What's Las Vegas got to do with it?" she said.

"I had to get you out of there, out of your condo."

*What?*

She shook her head as if to say she didn't understand.

He scooted even closer and took both of her hands in his. "Your condo is being scrubbed right now."

"Scrubbed. What?" She pulled her hands away. "What does that mean?"

"All of your things will be taken good care of, as if they were my own. Everything's going onto moving vans, which will be safely parked—until you make your decision."

She began to protest, but he cut her off.

"Devina, this is serious. It can't get out—about us. Your condo's going back on the market later today. We have to make you disappear."

"Why now? What happened to make you do this now? And why are we going to Vegas?"

"You've never been to Mission Valley, our meditation ranch. I thought this would be a good time to go. Give things a chance to settle down here. Get away for a few days. Get pampered. Massages. Five-star meals. Take a breather. Then we'll find a new place for you when we come back."

"I need my phone."

He closed his eyes and nodded. "We'll see to that."

The curtain opened. "Can I get you anything," the tall blond asked as she came over with her hands clasped in front of her.

"Strong coffee, please," Devina said.

"And you, Pastor Gentry?"

Hearing her call him that was sobering. Devina still couldn't believe Saul was the famous pastor she'd read about into the night.

Saul eyed his almost empty glass and looked as if he was debating on having another. But then he changed it up.

"I'll go back to coffee now, Sienna."

"Yes, sir." The flight attendant disappeared behind the curtain.

"Nothing has to change between us," he said.

"Ha, right. Answer my question. What happened to make you do this now?"

She had her suspicions, but she wanted to hear it from him.

He rubbed his face with his hands, then ran his fingers through his hair. He leaned back in his cushy seat with a sigh.

"Okay. A man from my congregation saw us together last night, leaving The Oyster. That's what triggered this."

*Hmm. Some truth.*

"Who? What man?" she pressed him, knowing full well it was Darren McQue, an extremely disgruntled former member of Vine & Branches Church.

"It doesn't matter."

"How do you know he's not going to blow the whistle on you?"

He froze and stared at her for the longest time. "This man won't talk. We're friends."

She knew they weren't friends anymore. In fact, they were enemies.

Something eerie passed between them, only for a split second, and it was gone. But it left Devina uneasy.

The flight attendant cleared her throat and came through the curtain with a tray containing two gold-rimmed cups of steaming coffee, cream, sugar, silver spoons, and cloth napkins. She set it on the small table and asked if she could get them anything else.

Saul mumbled no and waved her away.

"You don't have to live in Atlanta," he said. "You can live anywhere. Austin's a happening city. And I get there often because we have a location there. And I can make a point to get there more."

"I'm not leaving Atlanta."

"Fine. We'll find you a nice place. Maybe out a ways, near the Mall of Georgia. It'd be a lot closer for me. There's a lot going on there."

The thought of staying on Saul's payroll was enticing. What else would she do? Go back to working at Publix and living in a dump?

But what if Darren McQue did blow the whistle and expose Saul? The story would go viral. Devina would become infamous for being his call girl. She would be humiliated. Her parents would find out and their name would be sullied; their lives would be shattered.

The curtain opened once again, but this time a short, male pilot came through wearing navy slacks and a white button-down, short-sleeve shirt. He wore a captain's hat and had gold wings pinned to his left shirt pocket.

"Sir, good morning again." He nodded greetings toward Devina and glanced at his big watch. "We'll be leaving in about seven minutes. Clear skies expected all the way to Nevada. Flight time looks like about three hours and fifty-one minutes. We should touch down at about 10:55 a.m. Pacific time to a temperature of about ninety-three degrees."

"Whew," Saul said.

The pilot snickered. "Yes and the high will be about a hundred and four in Las Vegas today."

"Thanks, Howard," Gentry said, not bothering to introduce Devina.

Devina nodded at him.

"Good to have you aboard, Miss. Please let us know if there's anything we can do to make your flight more comfortable." With that he was gone, tossing the curtain like a magician tossing his cape.

Devina thought to herself that she could get used to this jet-setting lifestyle.

Saul's phone buzzed. He checked the screen, raised an eyebrow, and instantly stood and walked away from Devina to the other end of the cabin. He wore a crisp white dress shirt with gold cufflinks, light gray slacks, black shoes, and a black belt. He was an attractive man, but a troubled one. She saw no resemblance of the spiritual giant the magazines and tabloids had written about.

Saul paced and spoke in hushed tones. It appeared he may be arguing with whomever was on the phone. His voice got louder, just loud enough for Devina to hear.

"Did you offer what we talked about?" Saul said, then calmly waited for an answer. Someone spoke for a good twenty seconds on the other end, and Saul twisted and squeezed the back of his neck as he listened, then exploded with a string of expletives. A fist went to his mouth and he stalked back and forth, seemingly forgetting Devina was in the cabin.

"What now then?" he said, crossing to a wall of wood cabinets and leaning a hand against them while holding the phone to his ear and bending over to look out the window.

"I don't like it," he whispered.

The other person spoke.

"How?" he said. Then he lowered his voice more. "How would it be done?"

Saul listened intently.

He looked up at the ceiling of the cabin and ran his fingers through his hair, shaking his head. He listened. He paced. He thought.

"Do what you have to do. That's the last I want to hear about it."

He looked at the phone and jabbed a button to end the call.

Suddenly, he set his shoulders back and turned concisely and deliberately toward Devina, locking eyes with hers.

A wave of heat hit her, followed by a harrowing sense of dread.

*I need to get off this plane.*

There was a sudden bump and a loud hydraulic noise.

*No.*

The doors of the Gulfstream had closed.

A beep.

*Oh, no.*

The fasten seatbelt lights popped on.

*We're taking off.*

## TWENTY-FIVE

DARREN WAS GONE and although Nicole knew something had to be terribly wrong, she felt a subtle sense of peace guiding her as she took the cup of hot coffee to Detective Scottie Benson, who sat at the kitchen table with his legs crossed and an iPad in his lap. Benson appeared to be about fifty-five with thinning gray hair and a wide, solid five-foot-ten-inch frame.

"You said black?"

"Yes, please," said Benson, whose silver-rimmed eyeglasses were terribly smudged.

Nicole set the cup in front of him, pulled out the chair next to him and sat. They'd already tried Darren's phone again — and were sent to voicemail — and had covered the basics about Darren: age, date of birth, physical description, make and model of his car, license plate number, the last time they'd seen each other, and portions of what Becky Gentry had told Nicole about seeing Darren the night before.

"So, am I correct in thinking the last time you heard where Darren was, he was following this pastor, Neil Gentry, and the young lady who was with him? And you said he was on Piedmont?"

Nicole nodded. "Yes. On Piedmont almost to Midtown."

"And can you give me some context on why he was following these people?"

Nicole sighed. "This is a can of worms but let me try."

Over the next fifteen minutes, Nicole recapped her and Darren's history with Vine & Branches Church, Pastor Neil Gentry, the elders, and the whole sordid affair. She explained that Darren had been mad the day before about getting kicked out of Nicole's meeting with the elders, and that was probably why he went to Gentry's house the night before, and why he followed Gentry later that night.

Benson, who wore casual army green pants and a black polo shirt, was a very good listener—and he asked smart questions. He seemed as if he really cared about Darren's whereabouts, and not as if he was overworked, underpaid, and couldn't care less about the case, which is what Nicole had half expected.

"So, after all you guys have been through with this church, and this Pastor Gentry, it sounds like Darren may have hit the boiling point yesterday. Do you think that's accurate?"

"Maybe. I guess so," Nicole said. "And that's really not like him. He's not a violent person or anything like that."

"We talked briefly about your security camera. I know you said you don't know how to use it, but I know how to access the footage. We do it all the time with all kinds of cameras and software. And, while we're at it, I'd like to access Darren's credit cards online if I may, just to see if there's been any recent activity."

*Oh.*

Nicole hadn't thought of that. It stopped her cold. There wouldn't be charges Darren had made; he would never leave the girls. But there could be charges someone else had made, someone who had hurt Darren and stolen his credit cards.

Benson must have seen the worry on her face because he reached over and patted her wrist. "Don't worry. We're going to take this one step at a time. I'm here to help you. We'll figure it out."

A slew of emotions swirled and reached Nicole's eyes unexpectedly.

"Sorry." She got up. "Excuse me a second." She went into the guest bathroom, grabbed a tissue, wiped her eyes, and dabbed her nose as she checked herself in the mirror. She looked awful. *Thin. Pale ... Unhealthy.*

She did what she could with her hair, told herself this is how things were right now — that she would get back in shape later — and returned to the kitchen.

Benson was standing, finishing his coffee, looking out the window.

"Let's get on Darren's computer," Nicole said.

Benson turned around to face her.

"He has a file on there with all his passwords and websites and all that," she said. "Between the two of us, we should be able to figure it out."

THIRTY MINUTES LATER, sitting side-by-side at Darren's desktop computer in the cramped makeshift home office, Benson and Nicole looked at each other after visiting the third and final credit card website.

"Nothing," Nicole said.

"No," Benson said.

"Is that good or bad?"

Benson shrugged. "Can't say. It could rule out a robbery by some random thugs. They probably would've used the cards by now."

Nicole nodded. "He could have been in an accident."

"Well, we know he's not in any local hospitals. I told you I checked my sources on that."

"What if he's lying at the bottom of a ravine somewhere?"

"It's possible, not probable. There are so many people on the roads around here. Someone likely would have seen something and reported it or called for help — but I guess it could happen."

So, if it wasn't a random robbery or an accident, what did that leave?

Benson examined the many small icons on the glowing screen.

Nicole wanted to clean his glasses in the worst way but, of course, she didn't.

"Ah, here we go." Benson tilted his head back, peered through the bottom half of his glasses, and double-clicked an icon. "This is the app for your security cameras. Let's see what we can find."

"Like I said, that's all foreign to me. Darren's the tech guy."

"These things can be really useful," Benson said.

Darren's password came up automatically and soon Benson was working his way around the security camera website. Nicole told herself to try to remember what he was doing in case she ever needed to do it herself. He clicked 'History' and a long list of recent video clips dropped down. Each one showed the word 'Motion' and the time of day the motion occurred. There were recent times listed from that morning which must have been when Benson came to the door and, before that, when Becky had arrived and departed.

Benson moved the cursor and clicked one of entries on the list from the previous night.

The camera view opened up. It was a nighttime shot. The date and time stamp on the screen read August 12, 2024, 10:17 p.m.

*Last night.*

Benson clicked the big white arrow in the middle of the screen to play the video.

The camera setting was familiar. Darren, in his excitement about the app, had shown Nicole the camera view from above the front door when he'd installed it. And that's the same scene they were looking at now, only it was dark. The movement occurred when, way out past the front door, a dark four-door sedan pulled up in front of the house, stopped, and its lights went out.

"Is that car familiar to you?" Benson asked.

Nicole's heart rate spiked. She leaned closer to the screen and squinted. "No. I don't think so."

They watched in silence. No one got out of the car.

"It's hard to see," Nicole said. "Can you tell how many people are in the car?"

"At least two in the front."

The video ended.

"What happened?" Nicole said.

"It stopped due to lack of motion. Hold on."

Benson clicked the next video. It opened to the same setting.

Nighttime. The dark sedan parked out front with its lights out. Date and time stamp: August 12, 2024, 10:43 p.m.

Nicole did the math in her head. "So, this is twenty-six minutes later?"

"Correct."

A silver Honda Pilot drove slowly down the street, pulled around the parked sedan, and into the driveway.

"That's Darren!" Nicole said.

Just then, red and blue siren lights began flashing from inside the parked sedan.

"What?" Nicole murmured.

Darren stopped the Pilot right there, at the end of the driveway. His door opened and he got out.

Nicole's heart was thumping in her chest.

Darren took several steps toward the car with his hands out at his sides as if asking what was going on.

Two men got out of the dark car at the same time.

"That's not police," Benson said.

*No.*

The driver had on khakis and a dark button-down shirt, the other wore black cargo pants, a windbreaker, and a light-colored baseball cap.

One of them said Darren's name and Darren acknowledged him.

The volume was poor quality because they were so far from the camera.

"Can you turn it up?" Nicole said.

"It's as good as it will get. Shh."

Darren suddenly stopped when he was seven or eight feet from them and said, "You're not police."

The men ripped guns out at the same time, trained them on Darren, and walked toward him. "On your knees, on your knees." They repeated it, getting louder each time.

Finally, Darren slowly went to the ground.

He kept glancing at the house.

*He's thinking of the girls. Worried they would see. Worried they would come out.*

"We need you to come with us."

They approached Darren, one on each side, and lifted him up. The passenger with the cap pulled something from his coat pocket and turned Darren around.

*Handcuffs.*

Darren didn't seem to fight as the man snapped the cuffs on behind his back. Darren kept looking back toward the house.

"He wants them to get out of there—so they won't harm your children," Benson said with his eyes glued to the screen.

"Yes." Nicole whimpered.

The man with the cap pushed Darren toward the back of the sedan. The trunk popped open.

*No.*

The man forced Darren to sit on the edge of the trunk. He stared up at the house with eyes and mouth hanging open. It was a look of fright, but also of hope—for the girls. The man helped Darren into the trunk. It was so awkward with his hands locked behind him. The car bounced slightly when Darren dropped in. It had to hurt. The man shut the trunk quietly.

"Darren knew this would be captured on video," Nicole said.

"Yes," Benson said.

Meanwhile, the driver got back into the car. The siren lights stopped flashing.

The man wearing the cap hurried over to Darren's car and got in.

The dark sedan drove off.

The man in Darren's Pilot backed the car out quickly, stopped suddenly, and fishtailed slightly as he drove into the night.

## TWENTY-SIX

THE PREVIOUS NIGHT the driver had taken Darren to a house somewhere in Atlanta. Looking all around desperately as he was hoisted out of the trunk and led toward the house, he saw that it was an older neighborhood with middle- to upper-class houses of all shapes and sizes. They weren't the traditional houses that all looked similar in the suburban neighborhoods out where he lived. They were architecturally unique, ranging from one to five stories tall, with roofs at all angles, and odd-shaped windows. Darren guessed they were close to downtown Atlanta.

He figured the house they'd ended up in must've been an Airbnb or some kind of rental. The driveway had a huge crack in the middle, which caused it to be grossly misshapen. The house was ultra-modern but not kept up great. It was two stories with big windows. The inside featured contemporary colors and flooring materials, furniture, and light fixtures. He'd been taken to a tiny back bedroom on the main floor that had no windows, just a small, empty closet and a twin bed, nightstand, and lamp.

The only words spoken by the driver that night instructed Darren to stay in the room and get some sleep; he would be sorry if he opened the door. As the man spoke to Darren, he unlocked the handcuffs and allowed Darren to put his hands in front of him, where the cuffs were locked again.

Darren only slept a few minutes here and there through the

night. Many times he got up and walked to the door. Put his ear against it to listen. Came close to opening it but did not. He kept thinking that the front house camera at home would have picked up his abduction. The footage probably wouldn't have captured a license plate of the men's car because of the angle, but at least the car itself would have been caught on video, as well as the two men.

Lying on the bed early the next morning, staring up at the ceiling, he'd heard voices coming from the kitchen, near his room. He guessed the other man who'd abducted him had arrived.

Darren wondered what they had done with his car. He doubted the man would continue to drive it. By that time, hopefully the girls would have realized he was missing and called Nicole or the police. The man had probably ditched the Pilot somewhere and gotten a ride to this house.

Darren silently thanked God that the girls had been left alone. They would be okay.

Nicole would be there for them. She'd call the police. They would see the footage from the security camera.

He paused.

A strong wave of fear suddenly hit him and took his breath away.

*I may die today.*

A dark and eerie feeling echoed through his soul.

Never had he felt such a terrible and helpless sensation.

He became very anxious and began to squirm slightly there on the bed. It was hard to breathe. Like some kind of anxiety attack.

He closed his eyes and squeezed his hands together and told himself to be still.

*Calm me, God. Please, calm me.*

If he had minded his own business, he wouldn't be in this predicament. But Gentry had to be exposed. For Nicole's sake, the truth had to come out.

But would it?

Becky knew her husband had been riding around with another woman the night before. She had to be furious with him.

But would she be mad enough to do anything?

Gentry probably made up some lie about Devina, probably said she was some hurting church member.

Two hard knocks at the door startled him.

The door opened and Darren sat up.

The driver from the night before stepped into the room.

"I need to use the bathroom," Darren said.

The man nodded for him to get up.

Darren stood.

The man, who had dark brown hair and a scraggly brown beard, led Darren through the doorway into the hall and said, "First door on the right. Don't try anything. You see this." With that, the man turned his waist toward Darren so he could see the large black gun holstered on his wide leather belt.

"Can you take the cuffs off?" Darren held up his linked wrists.

"No way."

Darren managed anyway, then threw cold water on his face repeatedly and rinsed his mouth out and dried off. Over the sink, a nail stuck out of the wall where a mirror probably hung before. He guessed they took it down so he wouldn't break it and fashion a weapon.

He opened the door.

The man was right there. He took Darren by an arm and led him past the kitchen into a gathering room with two couches and a large coffee table. The other man from the night before sat at the end of one of the couches scrolling through his phone. He glanced up at Darren with sunburned cheeks and back down at the device.

Curtains were pulled closed against what he guessed was a large sliding glass door, and shades covered the various windows.

"Sit," said the man on the phone.

Darren sat on the couch opposite him.

His handler walked back to the kitchen and returned with a small white bag, which he dropped in Darren's lap.

It was from Popeye's.

Darren looked at both men who just stared at him.

He opened the bag, looked inside, then reached in and pulled out a sandwich. He unwrapped it. It was a sausage biscuit. He ate it ravenously.

"Here's the offer," said the man with the phone, who wore the same black cargo pants and windbreaker from the night before. His beige baseball cap was now on backwards. "Eighty thousand dollars will be given to you in payments of ten thousand a month for the next eight months. In exchange for the money, you will remain silent. Your wife will remain silent. She will stop any pursuit of any case against Pastor Gentry or the church. None of you will say another word about anything to anyone."

It was surreal.

Darren was being bribed by Pastor Neil Gentry.

"Oh," the man continued, "and you will move away from Atlanta, from Georgia, to another state—any other state—within two weeks."

*Can this really be happening?*

Darren crunched up the empty wrapper and stuffed it in the bag.

"If you accept these terms and *do not* remain silent, you and your whole family will pay the consequences," said the man with the baseball cap.

Darren's mind spun.

If he agreed to their terms now, in order to get out of there alive, then went to authorities, he and his family would die. He believed that now.

"Let me talk to Gentry," Darren said.

The man with the cap shook his head dramatically.

"I'm not going to accept blackmail," Darren said, hesitantly, fearfully.

The man in the cap threw up his hands and shrugged. "It's your call."

The driver said. "Take the money, dude. Live to see another day. You'd be a fool not to."

Darren bristled.

"What are you going to do to me—if I say no?"

The man with the cap looked down lazily, rolled his shoulders, took in a deep breath, and sighed loudly.

The driver said, "It's going to look like an accident."

## TWENTY-SEVEN

BECKY GENTRY WAS CRYING SO HARD she could barely see the road as she drove toward home.

She was fraught with anguish.

Nicole's words haunted her.

*Can it be true?*

She envisioned Neil and Nicole in an intimate setting, and Neil chuckling that prideful chuckle as he divulged private details about Becky's spending habits and her so-called desire to be a celebrity.

Becky was horrified.

Even if Neil did *think* those things, how dare he *share them* with anyone else, especially a woman he was . . . stalking.

It disgusted her.

*Is it true?*

Did Neil really go on and on with Nicole about Becky's attachment to fine things—her addiction to material things?

*How dare he!*

Becky screamed, "Noooo!" Then she whimpered, "This cannot be happening."

*It is true though.*

In her soul she knew they'd wandered far from God.

She was almost home but felt an urgency to pull over, to stop the car, to follow this train of thought before it vanished.

She did it.

Into the parking lot of an Auto Zone and into the first parking space she saw.

She threw the car into park and sobbed, pulled tissues from her purse, wiped her eyes and nose, knowing the things Nicole shared were true. And hating Neil for being the one to share those private observations.

Becky closed her eyes, dropped back against the seat, took in a huge breath, and exhaled. She did so three or four times.

The car was silent.

For a moment, time stood still.

She embraced the quiet. She never had quiet anymore.

"God . . . we are so far from you."

That was the truth. *Finally*. The truth.

But it was only Becky who was feeling it.

Not Neil.

They were worlds apart.

He'd grown so far from God it was pitiful.

In fact, if all the allegations were true, she didn't even know the man.

It sickened her to think of all he may have done with those women.

*And shame on you,* Becky thought.

She'd overlooked Neil's lies. Gone along with everything. Kept it going with him. Pretended not to hear the rumors. Instead of confronting them head on like she should have, she'd ignored them, just kept moving at a hundred miles an hour. Took her mind off Neil's alleged improprieties by getting lost in luxury and fine things, material things that never ended up satisfying her. And, yes, the blueprints for the new lake house—the show place.

She remembered back when they were just starting the church. They were so young and excited. She worked with Neil getting the church off the ground, overseeing the nursery, creating the church bulletin and newsletter, keeping track of visitors. Then, when the kids were born, she stayed home with them. Neil worked twelve-to-fourteen-hour days and made next to nothing in pay. He borrowed money from his parents to make ends meet. Yet, they were so happy. Sharing God with others was all that mattered. It was what had fueled them. As those first families joined Vine & Branches, they formed a close-knit community; it felt even closer than family.

It was right when the church began to explode in size that Nicole and Darren had become part of that family. They had been genuinely close. She knew in her heart they were good people.

Becky sat there in a daze and stared at nothing for a long time. Those days were so far gone.

What was she feeling?

*Guilt.*

As if she had dozens of priorities and God was nowhere on the list.

She never allowed herself to think like this anymore. Never had a moment to contemplate such things. Always filled her time with the kids, the new house, the church, clothes . . .

She was running.

Running from God.

Running from Neil's . . . indiscretions.

Self-medicating by spending and focusing on how she could improve her life.

But, if the way they were living was so wrong, if Neil was guilty, why was God still growing Vine & Branches?

Maybe that had been her mistake. She'd always used the growth of the church as a litmus test to determine how well she — they — were doing spiritually. Neil had *always* played that card.

She was sick of it.

And she was humiliated!

How could she have let it get to this point?

He was a flirt and a liar!

What people must think of her for supporting him through it all.

She thought of the necklace in her purse. She was almost positive it was the one he'd given Nicole as a Christmas present.

The thought of it was too maddening to dwell on.

If she were to expose Neil, it would be the end of life as they knew it.

He would fall.

So would she.

The big income. The houses. The cars. The limitless spending. *Gone.*

She let her head drop to her chest.

"God, you are what matters." The tears came suddenly and the tide of emotion took her breath away. "I'm sorry for all I've done to let you down. Forgive me, please . . . restore me to you. Restore our relationship."

She thought of the kids. They'd already heard the rumors and allegations. They had to be questioning what was going on with their father.

The truth would come out, whatever it was, and they'd all have to live with it, deal with it, put it behind them, and move on.

It was time. She nodded, feeling a refreshing sense of urgency.

She and Neil were supposed to have dinner together that night.

But this couldn't wait.

She grabbed her purse and dug out her phone. She would call Neil's personal secretary, Wendy, and find out where he was. She would go right now, with the necklace, and confront him. She would not back down until the truth came out. It would start between them, and they would decide how to move forward.

The phone vibrated in her hands.

She looked at the screen.

It was a text message from Neil.

She set her resolve and read the message:

> Hey babe. I wanted to give you a heads-up that I'm en route to Vegas. We have a chance to acquire property adjacent to MVR. I'm meeting the property owner to discuss. Shouldn't be out there long. Love you.

Becky turned off the phone, sighed, and closed her eyes.

She wondered if that was really where he was going.

She wondered if there was a woman involved.

There was a hitch in her breathing.

She pictured Mission Valley Resort in Las Vegas. The plush rooms. The pool and spa. The sunshine and cactus and palm trees. The fine dining.

## CELEBRITY PASTOR

The perfect place to meet someone.
Becky had been there many times.
She knew the ropes.
This couldn't wait any longer.
She called the airline.

## TWENTY-EIGHT

DEVINA SAT across from Neil and was looking pensive, as she had ever since they'd taken off from PDK several hours ago. She had her earbuds in and was reading something on her Kindle, or at least pretending to. She'd only made brief eye contact with Neil several times and those appeared to have been accidental on her part.

*She's scared.*

That wasn't good, Neil thought.

None of what was happening was good.

Neil had to weather this storm. Had to.

He thought of the suffering Darren McQue must have gone through, or was about to go through, and shivered.

Apparently Badger had a small team of . . . experts.

Devereux always knew what he was doing, and Neil took some comfort in the fact that it was Devereux who had found Badger. Devereux had never failed him yet.

*He better not start now.*

It was always dangerous bringing new people into the inner circle.

Neil looked out the round window and saw only white clouds far below as the Gulfstream cruised smoothly at a steady altitude of 41,000 feet.

This was the lifestyle he deserved.

He sipped the fresh coffee Sienna had brought out and thought how odd it was that he had chosen the alias Saul Dagon, as Devina had pointed out. Devina had actually read the scriptures—about Saul, Dagon, and David. It dawned on Neil that, by having Darren . . . removed from the picture, he was doing exactly what King David had done when he'd arranged for Bathsheba's husband to be killed.

He couldn't think about it.

That wasn't him doing that. It was out of his hands.

He thought of what Devina had said she'd read about Dagon, the false god, repeatedly falling, then finally crashing so hard that his arms and legs broke off.

*Don't think about it.*

He glanced at his phone. The jet had wi-fi, of course. But he had not heard back from Becky after he'd texted her that he was heading to Vegas. Oh well, she was still upset from last night. Neil shook his head, thinking about how badly he'd been busted. For Ron Sawyer to call Becky—it had been uncanny timing.

*Unbelievable.*

But could it possibly be more than unbelievably bad luck?

Could God be intervening?

*Interfering* would be a better word.

And why all the sudden had Darren decided to show up at their house, and then follow Neil later. And find him—with Devina!

The old spiritual side of Neil would say none of it was coincidence.

There were no such things as coincidences to the devout Christian.

Everything was scripted out by an omniscient God.

The same God who let Neil's brother drown when they were boys.

Neil felt himself scowling.

He'd become so cold, so negative.

Just then, Devina's eyes flicked up at him. They made eye contact, and her eyes darted back down to her Kindle.

Neil snapped his fingers and waved a hand at her. She tapped the screen of the Kindle several times and looked up at him. He signaled for her to take her earbuds out.

She removed one of them and looked at him with eyebrows raised and a smart aleck look on her face.

"The best sushi restaurant in the country is within ten minutes of our resort," Neil said, waiting for a positive response.

Devina closed her eyes and slumped her shoulders.

She shook her head.

"Oh, that's right," he said, feeling like an idiot. "You don't like seafood."

She did not look up again, but simply plugged the earbud back into her ear.

Neil's face ignited. He felt his nostrils flare.

*You ungrateful, money hungry, gold digger!*

How dare she treat him like that.

He shot up from his seat and snatched his phone from the armrest.

Devina did not look up but shifted uncomfortably in her seat.

Neil stalked past her to the farthest seat away, a long leather couch that ran perpendicular with the aisle of the jet. He plunked down at the far end, crossed a leg, and composed a text message to Spencer Devereux:

> Have Devina's room bugged at MVR.

Devereux usually always responded quickly to any text from Neil and, sure enough, he wrote back within seconds:

> OK. What's going on?

Neil groaned, tilted his head back, and looked up to the ceiling of the jet, thinking of the most concise way to put it. He texted back to Devereux:

> I think she's spooked.

Devereux's response was immediate:

Spooked?

Neil cursed and typed back:

Never mind. Just do it!

∼

BECKY WAS SWEATING and in a crazy rush as she tossed several days' worth of clothing and toiletries into an overnight bag.
*God, help me make this flight.*
She'd arranged for Savannah to babysit Eli and Hazel—and Savannah's mom even offered to have the kids stay at their house, which was better yet.
*People do anything for the great Pastor Neil Gentry.*
But that was all about to change.

∼

DARREN SAT in silence in the living room of the rental house, praying repeatedly: *God, get me out of this.*
The two men were talking quietly in the kitchen.
Darren was so nervous he thought he might throw up.
Weighing on his mind most were Dottie and Dixie—and Nicole. He wasn't ready to leave them. Most of all, it made him sick to think of them without a father and husband. He hadn't planned well enough for that. He always thought he would have more time for that as he got older. At least he had a decent life insurance policy and a bit of money in savings.
Nicole would make it. She would take good care of the girls and raise them right. She had been an amazing mother. In light of his current circumstances, Darren wished he had forgiven her. He looked at his hand and wished he'd never taken off his wedding ring. She'd admitted her mistakes and had asked his forgiveness multiple times. And besides, look at the demon she had been up against. A man who was about to have Darren murdered.
What were his options now? He could take the bribe. They

could move. Him, Nicole, and the girls. Start over. Go to Charlotte or Raleigh. But Darren knew deep down that if he did that, it would eventually be found out. Pastor Neil Gentry was going to be exposed, sooner or later. And Darren and Nicole would be guilty of accepting an eighty-thousand-dollar bribe. They would be part of it.

The other option . . . well, there would be no trying to fight these two men; they both had big guns and they were both roughneck thugs. They would pulverize him in a fight. He'd already watched breathlessly for opportunities to run, but there had been none, not even close. He would continue to watch vigilantly for the right opportunity, thinking running was his best bet.

What had they meant when they had said they were going to make it look like an accident? Would they shoot him in this room and put the gun in his hand to make it look like a suicide? Or hang him in the garage? Or give him pills to make it look like an overdose?

He considered telling the men they were caught on camera back at his house, telling them there was no way they would get away with killing him.

The two men walked back into the living room where Darren was seated.

"What's it going to be?" said the man in the baseball cap.

Darren didn't hesitate. "I can't take the bribe."

Both men shook their heads and sighed. They went back into the kitchen and had words. Then the man in the cap made a call while the other man took a seat across the room from Darren in a straight back chair, which he leaned back at a forty-five-degree angle. He scrolled through the phone endlessly.

*God, turn their evil in upon themselves. Help me get out of this.*

At least if they killed Darren, he would be in heaven. He knew that. But he'd never been so close to that reality.

The guy in the kitchen ended his call and dropped his phone in his back pocket as he approached Darren.

"Get up. We're going."

Darren's stomach turned. He stood. His head spun. He

gripped the back of the chair to steady himself. "I think I'm going to be sick."

The other man banged his chair upright, stood, and yelled, "Get to the bathroom!"

Darren ran to it, shut the door, and bent over the toilet.

He threw up what he'd just eaten, and his throat burned from the acid of his stomach.

Sweating profusely, he spun the toilet roll, ripped off a bunch of tissue, and swabbed his face and forehead with it.

He dry-heaved several times, thinking that the top of the porcelain toilet tank would make a good weapon. But there was just no way. What was he going to do, lure them in there one at a time?

"Let's go," one of the men yelled, then banged on the wall three times.

*I've got to get away—for the girls.*

He opened the door and went back out, thinking he would try to run when they got outside. Thinking, if he could just stay alive long enough, the police would track down these men, their car.

"Okay, let's move," said the man who'd been on the phone.

They began walking toward the door.

The man wearing the cap led the way with Darren behind him, followed by the other man. When they got to the door, the brown-haired guy stopped and turned around just two feet from Darren.

"Don't try anything."

He pushed the door open.

The sunlight made Darren squint and put a hand above his eyes.

It was a beautiful, sunny, breezy day.

They walked down the sidewalk to the driveway and Darren stopped in his tracks.

His silver Honda Pilot was sitting there, along with the black, older model four-door Dodge Avenger they'd kidnapped him in.

Darren understood the plan now.

They were going to wreck his car—with him in it.

# TWENTY-NINE

Nicole knew she should eat something. It was past lunch time. But the thought of food made her stomach twist in knots.

Before he'd left the house, Detective Benson had put out two all-points bulletins—one on Darren's Honda and another on the dark colored Dodge in which he'd been abducted. He'd also promised to call Nicole the minute he knew anything more.

Dottie and Dixie were still at school and Nicole had called Sheryl Ferguson and asked if she could pick them up and bring them home later that afternoon.

Nicole checked her phone again.

Nothing from Darren.

She tried to call him again and was sent straight to voicemail.

She plunked down in a chair in the family room.

Darren was such a good man. He'd been such a solid husband and father. The girls adored him.

All this was her fault.

How could she have been so stupid, so weak to fall for the advances of Neil Gentry?

She hated herself for it.

The man was so full of himself. Overly independent. Never wanting to share the ministry spotlight with anyone else. Always using his sermons and his fancy Greek and Hebrew translations to flatter himself, to make him look like some high and lofty scholar. Always turning the conversation back to himself. Often unapproachable and surrounded by his entourage. People were tools to him, and in her case, they were toys. She remembered the times she'd seen him respond to the slightest criticism with self-defense and even anger.

Her head dropped to her chest and she cried.

*Where are you, Darren?*

If something had happened to him, if he was hurt, she could never forgive herself. No, she never would. No psychologist could convince her otherwise.

Her phone rang and she jumped. She'd turned the volume up to make sure she wouldn't miss a call.

She looked at the screen.

*Oh no.*

Darren's mom, Sheila, was calling.

*How can she know something is wrong so fast?*

Sheila and Nicole hadn't spoken since Nicole had moved out. Nicole was sure Sheila blamed her for the whole mess.

Nicole couldn't put her off. She answered the call.

"Nicole, it's Sheila. Do you know where Darren is? I've been trying to reach him all day. It's not like him not to get back to me."

*Oh boy, here we go.*

Nicole explained everything right up to the details about Detective Benson's involvement and the security footage they'd watched of Darren's abduction.

Sheila was aghast.

Her words were choppy and filled with rage.

Nicole was up now, wandering the house, fielding her mother-in-law's questions as best she could.

"You're telling me you think the pastor of that church—the one you had an affair with—is behind Darren's disappearance? It's preposterous."

Once Sheila calmed down somewhat, she inquired about the girls. She then insisted she was going to make the trip over there, to be with the girls, to help Nicole, and to wait for word on Darren.

Nicole could not refuse her. She didn't want Sheila there, but she owed it to her. They needed to face each other sometime. And she might be needed to watch the girls. She lived an hour away. Her husband, Darren's dad, had passed away about six years ago.

So it was settled. Sheila would be there within a few hours. They ended the call.

Nicole went upstairs to the linen closet and got out fresh towels and sheets to make the guest bed and get things ready.

The girls would be glad Sheila was there. They loved her.

Once the bed was made and the towels were set out nicely, Nicole decided to drive back to her apartment and get her dirty laundry. She would bring it back and do it at the house instead of the sketchy laundromat, and it would give her something to help pass the time while she waited on word about Darren.

~

ONCE SEATED in her first-class seat on the Delta flight to Las Vegas, Becky Gentry pulled the seatbelt tight and let out a huge sigh of relief.

She checked the time on her phone.

She looked out the window.

She did the math.

She should arrive at Mission Valley Resort only a few hours after Neil.

He was in for a surprise.

~

DARREN WALKED AS SLOWLY as the two men would allow him toward his Honda Pilot, but his insides were firing on all cylinders. He needed to make a split-second decision whether to run or not.

He frantically scanned the area.

Being out in the open air, seeing daylight and reality, Darren thought surely the police would find these cars, find him.

"Let's go." The man behind him with the stringy brown hair spoke in a low, mean voice, shoving him as he did so.

Darren still wore the handcuffs in front.

The woods on both sides of the long, cracked driveway were

too thick and uneven to attempt to run through. He would trip and fall, and they'd have him. If he tried this, he would sprint down the driveway, which was about sixty yards long, and turn right when he got to the road. He would be in broad daylight. There were plenty of houses around. Hopefully someone would see him running, see the men chasing him, perhaps even with their guns drawn—and call the police.

If he didn't try now, he may not get another chance.

Once they put him in his car, he may never get out.

His ears roared.

The brightness seared even brighter.

His head seemed to float above the desperate scene.

He took off.

The men both cussed behind him.

He ran—as fast as he could down the driveway.

*Get to the street.*

The men's angry voices were farther away now.

"I'll take his car, you go on foot," one yelled.

"Don't shoot him. It's got to be an accident."

As Darren got to the road and turned right, a sense of horror consumed him when he heard one of the cars rev to life behind him.

A woman approached on the left side of the neighborhood street. She was older, blond, wearing a knee brace, walking her little dog very slowly.

"Call the police," Darren yelled as he sprinted past her, "I've been kidnapped. Darren McQue . . . that's my name."

Darren looked back, hoping the men hadn't heard him.

The man with the cap was catching up to him on foot.

And the car, Darren's car, was coming.

He could only hope that lady heard him clearly and would call the police.

Surely, she would. She saw the handcuffs.

*She sees them chasing me.*

Knowing the car would catch him if he stayed on the road, Darren looked for an alternative, an out, as he continued to run as fast as he could. Panting. Sweating. Feeling himself slowing.

*God . . . please.*

He heard the man's footsteps behind him, his heavy breathing, cursing.

Darren searched for somewhere to go, anywhere.

There were only driveways and houses. No side streets. The woods were no good.

The car roared from behind—so thunderous Darren swore he felt the heat from it.

The man was only steps behind him.

Darren heard him grunt as he lunged.

He was *on* Darren.

Everything spun.

Darren couldn't break his fall because of the handcuffs.

But, as they went down, Darren turned his body at the last second, getting his captor underneath him and landing on him as hard as he could as they smashed the road.

The wind went out of the man with a horrid noise.

The back of Darren's head cracked the pavement. But he scrambled to his feet.

The other man rolled over to his hands and knees and fought to get a breath.

The Pilot was suddenly there, turning within five feet of him. It screeched to a halt. The driver was out in seconds with his gun drawn.

Darren could only hold his cuffed hands in front of him.

His arms were bleeding.

He felt blood dripping down the back of his neck.

The elderly woman who was walking her dog, who was surely going to call the police, was in the back seat.

# THIRTY

IN THE COOL limo on the way to Mission Valley Resort, Devina sat as far apart as she could from Pastor Neil Gentry.

She had decided on the Gulfstream's approach to Las Vegas McCarran International Airport that she had had enough—she was done playing Neil Gentry's game. As he had sat sulking over on one of the jet's leather couches, she made up her mind that she couldn't live like this anymore. The man was a dishonest liar and a user. He'd cheated on his wife, and in Devina's mind, that meant he'd cheated on his kids and his church as well. He'd used Devina. And that made her feel dirty—and guilty.

She didn't want to feel that way anymore.

And the whole episode with Badger showing up, 'scrubbing' her condo, taking her phone.

*Nope.*

It all gave her the creeps.

Nothing was worth living the lie she had been living. Not the condo. Not the clothes. Nothing. She wasn't going to be used anymore.

All she wanted right now was to get back to Atlanta. To go home. She would go to her mom and dad's house. A safe place where she could get back on her feet. That's all she wanted and her mind was made up.

The trick was going to be making a clean exit.

The phone call she'd heard Saul make earlier while they were still in the air had been disturbing. It led her to believe Darren McQue may be in trouble, at Saul's hand. Someone like Badger may have been sent to stop him from talking.

As if that wasn't scary enough, Devina was beginning to wonder what Saul may do to her if she didn't go along with his plan to keep her mouth shut and remain his mistress.

"What are you thinking about?" Saul's words from across the limo's wide back seat woke her out of her daydream.

"Oh." She had to think fast. "Ever since you mentioned a massage, that's all I can think about." Devina had to play the game and keep it all positive while she pulled the wool over his eyes.

"Well, that's the first thing we're going to do, then." Saul went into a long dissertation about the spa and all of the fine amenities at Mission Valley Resort. As he did so, Devina replayed in her mind the email she'd sent when they had been in the air.

Although Badger had taken her phone away, what Saul didn't realize was that Devina could still access the internet on her Kindle. In doing so, she'd found the name of the reporter from *The Washington Post* who had written the investigative pieces about Pastor Neil Gentry and Vine & Branches Church. Devina emailed the man, Horace Stone, anonymously using an email address that didn't give her name away. She told him she had damning inside information about Pastor Neil Gentry and asked for Stone's cell phone number.

"Devina?" Saul said.

"What? I'm sorry." Devina looked over at him across the shiny black seat, the tinted windows darkening the sunny Nevada day and rocky landscape passing by outside.

"I asked if Indian food sounded good for dinner," he snapped. "You didn't hear me?"

"Oh, yeah, no, I heard you. Indian is fine. I'm going to need a nap at some point."

"What did I say about it?" Saul sounded annoyed. "About the Indian food."

Devina swallowed hard, not liking the tone of his voice. She took a guess. "You know of a good place for authentic Indian food in Vegas. I'm looking forward to it."

"What's the name of it?"

"I can't pronounce it," she lied, not knowing the name.

"You need to tune in more when I speak to you."

*What? This is flat out weird.*

Just confirmation that she needed out.

She found herself just staring at him, wondering what on earth she was doing there. Wondering how she could have let herself get hoodwinked by this . . . fraud.

"Let's work on that," Saul said, then got his phone out to look busy.

Devina sat there in shock. As the seconds ticked by, she got angrier and angrier.

*How dare he talk to me like that.*

She got her Kindle out of her bag and turned it on.

Once it came to life she swiped the screen.

There was an email notification.

Her heart rate kicked up.

She clicked it on.

Horace Stone had returned her email. He'd given his phone number and a quick note, "Call any time, day or night."

"What are you reading?" Saul's voice broke the silence.

*Now he's trying to make nice? He's totally unstable.*

Devina turned and stared at him.

"I guess you'd call it a psychological thriller."

# THIRTY-ONE

Nicole had rounded up the dirty laundry at her apartment and was driving back to the house, dreading having Darren's mom coming to stay. She checked the time. The kids would be getting home from school in a while. With every minute that went by, she felt more worried about what had happened to Darren.

She couldn't wait any longer and called Detective Scottie Benson on the speakerphone in her car. He picked up right away.

"I'm sorry Mrs. McQue, nothing yet," he said.

"You can call me Nicole."

"Okay, Nicole. I promise, when I know anything, you will hear from me directly."

She thanked him, hung up, and turned into the neighborhood.

For about the third time since it had happened, she regretted how bluntly and candidly she'd spoken to Becky Gentry that morning when she'd told her what Neil had confided to her about Becky's big spending habits and desire to be in the limelight. Nicole recalled the painful look on Becky's face. The betrayal. The hurt. The anguish.

"I shouldn't have done that," Nicole whispered as she pulled in the driveway. She parked in the garage and got the laundry basket out of the back.

As she walked toward the door to the house, inside the garage, she heard a car pull into the driveway behind her, surprised Sheila had made it there so quickly.

She glanced back out toward the driveway.

It wasn't Sheila.

It was Spencer Devereux in his red Mercedes SUV.

"What the heck does he want?" she mumbled.

She set the basket at the door, walked past her car toward the driveway, and stood in front of Devereux's expensive car with her arms crossed.

Nicole wondered if Devereux had news about Darren. Or would he even say he knew Darren was missing?

Devereux finished a phone call and got out of the car.

"Nicole," he nodded and approached her, wearing dark blue skinny jeans, a white shirt, and black Converse sneakers.

"What can I do for you?" Nicole said formally.

"I came by to see Darren, is he around?"

*Hmm.*

Nicole wasn't about to give this guy anything.

"He's not here."

"Oh . . . Okay. If you will, tell him I stopped by to see him."

"What's it about, Spencer?"

"It can wait." He waved a hand and headed back to his car.

"Tell me what it's about." Nicole walked closer to him.

Devereux stopped between the open driver's door and the car. He smiled, and stared at her, and tried to sound nonchalant. "It's okay. I'll catch him later."

"You don't have any business with him," Nicole said sharply. "You kicked him out of the meeting yesterday. He's not part of the church. Why are you doing this?" She was thinking he may have come there to give himself an alibi in Darren's disappearance. *Covering his behind.*

Devereux held up both hands as if surrendering. "I wasn't going to say anything to you since you already have enough on your plate with the investigation and all."

"I'm a big girl."

"Well, the truth is, we've discovered that there are some major funds missing from the coffee shop ministry."

Nicole felt her face ignite and her ears roared with static.

"Have him call me, will you?" He got in his car and slammed the door.

She glared at him with what felt like fire blazing from her eyes.

He smirked as he put the car in reverse and backed out.

# THIRTY-TWO

WHENEVER PASTOR NEIL GENTRY showed up in person at Mission Valley Resort, his meditation ranch outside of Las Vegas, the staff and administrators bubbled over with excitement. It was no different this day. And, since it wouldn't look good if Pastor Gentry showed up with another woman besides his wife Becky, whom the staff also adored, Pastor Gentry had instructed Devina to go with Morris, the chief of staff at MVR, who had met them at the limo. With the help of an acne-faced teenage bellboy dressed in black, Morris quietly brought Devina in a side door and showed her to her private quarters on the top floor and let her know Pastor Gentry had arranged a massage for her.

Meanwhile, in the main lobby, MVR employees circled around Gentry as he proudly took center stage and presented an upbeat, impromptu state-of-MVR speech, commenting on how much extensive and positive press the resort had been receiving of late, and how well the resort had been performing financially.

Pam Friend, the small, round, thirty-something director of communications at MVR, was pink with embarrassment as a result of Gentry's praise. She had arranged for a photographer and videographer to be on hand to capture Pastor Gentry's visit. As employees came up to Gentry after his speech to let him know they were reading his latest book or to tell him how much they'd loved his newest sermon series, photos and videos were shot with lots of handshakes, hugs, and laughter.

Meanwhile, Pam Friend disappeared for a few minutes and came back, whispering to Pastor Gentry that there was a phone call for him on the house line.

Gentry squinted at her and cocked his head. "The house line? Who is it?"

"Uhh . . . a Mr. Badger," Friend said.

Gentry swallowed hard and sobered. "Where can I take it?"

"Follow me, sir."

After Gentry shook hands and took selfies with a few more employees, he followed Friend into an office behind the marble counter in the lobby. She pointed to a phone that was off the hook resting on a desk. Two employees, a young man and woman, were busy with office work.

Gentry glanced at Pam Friend and said, "I'll need the room."

"Sasha and Jeremy, please let Pastor Gentry have some privacy for his call."

The two looked at each other, then at Pastor Gentry, smiling and nodding as they humbly gathered a few things in their arms and scurried out of the room, smiling in adoration as they left.

Friend nodded at Pastor Gentry and closed the door as she left.

He looked around to make sure the room was empty, then he picked up the phone. "Yo, go."

"Sir, it's Badger. I didn't want to use a cell phone due to the private nature of this call."

"Where are you?"

"I just landed in Vegas, sir. I'll be heading to MVR soon. But there's been a bit of a . . . hiccup."

Gentry shut his eyes, squeezed his forehead, and sighed angrily.

"Darren McQue ran from my team," Badger said.

Gentry's heart seemed to smash his rib cage.

"Don't worry, they caught him. But an elderly woman saw him running. My men were forced to . . . detain her."

*No.*

*No, no, no.*

"What do you mean, 'detain her'?"

He swallowed hard, dreading what he was about to hear.

"They were afraid she was going to blow everything, so they have her now. With Darren McQue."

Gentry ripped the phone away from his ear and shook it repeatedly. His face contorted. He clenched his teeth and smacked the phone on the desk four or five times.

*This cannot be happening. No one was ever supposed to get hurt.*

Gentry cursed at Badger. "You should have taken your chances and left her alone!" he hissed. "You said she's an old lady. Now you've *kidnapped* her. You've made it *worse*."

"Sir, to clarify, she saw him running from my men in broad daylight, with handcuffs on. They think he may have even yelled at her to call the police. We could not leave that thread dangling. If we had—"

"You don't need to spell it out for me. I understand what happened. But it's on you that he ran. He shouldn't have ever had that opportunity. I gave you one job. One job!"

Silence.

"Sir, I apologize. Let's just try to keep our cool—"

Gentry's whole body swayed, and he saw stars he was so furious.

"You miserable little . . . how dare you tell me to keep my cool!"

Gentry's face was an inferno. He paced back and forth as far as the cord would stretch, with the phone smashed to his ear. He could barely breathe. He was sweating profusely. He couldn't think straight. He didn't feel like himself. His mind raced. He felt out of control, as if he was floating above the room.

"We can make this right, sir." Badger's voice sounded distant. "I have a plan."

It was all coming down on Gentry, caving in, smothering him.

The wrongness of it all—of everything. Devina. Nicole. The other women. Cheating on Becky. All the money, the fraud. All the houses and cars. All the lies.

And now this.

"Sir?" Badger said. "Can you hear me?"

*Look who you're working with . . . what you're doing.*

Gentry forced himself to breathe.

He was trembling terribly.

He looked at the door. He couldn't let them see him like this. He had to pull it together. He wiped the sweat from his face with the arm of his jacket, which came away with dark wet spots.

Was this a panic attack? Heart attack?

*God's punishing you. He's had enough.*

*You need to confess. Repent. Step down.*

He could see the dark, viral headlines and news reels about the scandalous collapse; the hurt and outrage in Becky's eyes; the murmuring and judgement that would blaze through Vine & Branches like wildfire; the disappointment and possible rebellion in Eli and Hazel; the endless police investigations; the trials and jail time.

*You're too far in.*

Gentry cleared his throat, took a deep breath, and spoke to Badger quietly and slowly. "Where are they now?"

"Together. With my men. I wanted to consult with you before proceeding. We can make this right. We can go ahead with the accident."

"What about her?" Gentry's voice suddenly cracked with emotion.

"She needs to disappear. We can make that happen. It is not a problem. I assure you. She will never be seen or heard from again."

The words echoed in Gentry's head.

A gloomy sense of dread flooded his soul. His dark soul.

*What are you thinking?*

He could go to prison, for a long time.

"And we won't charge any extra," Badger said, "since it was our mistake, and we want this to be a long-term partnership."

*Fool.*

Gentry paced.

"Sir?"

"I'm thinking."

Gentry always worked things out. He was the golden boy. There were never any problems too big. If the old woman is removed, and Darren McQue dies in a car accident, everything is fine. The only remaining threat is Devina, and her room is bugged.

"Badger."

"Yes, sir."

"Do as you planned. I never want to hear another word about it. Text me when you arrive at MVR. Ask for Morris. He'll have a room for you."

"Affirmative."

Gentry hung up the phone and looked around for a mirror.

## THIRTY-THREE

Becky Gentry felt somewhat out of her mind as her flight touched down in Las Vegas. With trepidation, she grabbed her overnight bag, deplaned, and rented a car—all seamlessly. She got outside and was instantly hit by Nevada's mid-day summer heat. She wheeled her bag to spot number five, a light gray GMC Terrain SUV, got in, and cranked the AC.

The cold air blew hard on her face, and she dropped back in the seat, leaned her head back against the headrest, closed her eyes, and prayed for God to carry her. It was all up to him now. She was surrendered.

She had to keep going with this plan. Move forward. One step at a time. No more denial. No more lies. No more covering up the sins. She leaned forward. Her hair blew back as she searched Mission Valley Resort on the car's GPS—a twenty-two-minute drive.

Before heading out, she dug the necklace out of her purse—the one Neil supposedly gave to Nicole McQue as a Christmas gift. She studied it in the palm of her hand, the broken silver chain, the brown leather disc, the mod silver cross. Little did Neil know she had ended up with it. He certainly must wonder what had happened to it. Becky reached for her phone, found Nicole in her contacts, opened a text to her, snapped a photo of the necklace, and wrote:

> Is this the necklace Neil gave you?

She put the necklace in her pocket, set the phone aside, and got going, maneuvering her way through the parking lot, over the strip of flat spikes, down an access road, and onto the highway.

A text came back from Nicole:

> Yes.

Becky blinked and looked at the text again, just to make sure.
Something seeped from Becky's soul.
Neil was not the man she thought he was.
*How could he do this? To me. The kids. God.*
She'd known. Deep down, somewhere very deep down, she'd known.
She'd glossed over it. She'd moved so fast and kept so busy . . . that was how she had coped.
*God, how far away from you we've fallen.*
She talked to herself as she drove, going over all the lies and coverups. She cursed and cried and yelled and questioned how much she was at fault—not for Neil's nasty affairs—but for being hypnotized by the fame and wealth.
And what about Darren McQue? The thought of him being missing almost took her breath away. Becky had told Neil the night before that Darren had followed him and that young girl.
Could Neil have done something to Darren? Could her very own husband be that cruel, that evil?
*Where is Darren?*
Suddenly, Becky wondered if *she* might be in danger.
*No.*
Neil would never do anything to jeopardize the appearance that their marriage was anything but a bed of roses.
But that lie was about to be exposed.
Once she was settled in at MVR, Becky would show Neil the necklace. She would also confront him with all the derogatory things Nicole told her Neil had said about her. Every hurtful thing. She would find out the truth about the young black girl he had been with the night before. She would press him on his sexual

advances toward Brenda Vincent, former worship leader at Vine & Branches and the first person to speak out about Neil's misconduct. She would insist on knowing the truth about the other women. And she would find out if Neil knew where Darren was.

Her biggest concern in all of this was the kids. How they would take it. How it would affect them at school, their relationships. How they would move forward as a single-parent family. They'd already heard the rumors; how could they not? Becky would be there for them. She could handle it. She didn't know where they would end up living, but the three of them would be a family. And they would put God back where he belonged—as the centerpiece of their lives.

---

THE TWO MEN were out of breath and furious. The fact that Darren had run had forced them to take another prisoner, the elderly woman now seated beside him on the orange couch back at the rental house. Her dainty, age-spotted hands were tied in front of her with zip ties and she was shaking so violently her teeth were chattering.

"Why'd we come back here?" yelled the man with the dark brown hair and scraggly beard. "People are going to see us coming and going."

The men were losing their cool, which gave Darren the smallest spark of hope—as if he had managed to penetrate their stoic, killer-style professionalism.

"What else were we gonna do? We didn't plan on this." The man in the beige cap waved toward the lady. "I had to talk to Badger."

*Badger.*

Darren racked his brain trying to recall anyone by that name, but it was not familiar to him.

Darren was hurting. His arms and the back of his head were still bleeding. The men weren't about to do anything about that.

"Well now you've talked to him. What are we doing? What's the plan?"

The poor woman, a thin little gal with curly blond hair and a black knee brace, was mumbling about her dog not having anyone. From what Darren could gather, she was a widow and the dog had been left in the street when they'd abducted her.

Darren could only hope a neighbor saw all that and called the police.

"What's your name?" Darren whispered in hopes of soothing her.

"Doris," she whispered back, followed by a big swallow.

"I'm Darren."

They looked steadily at each other, and Darren found only desperation in her blue eyes.

"Don't be afraid, Doris. God has us. It'll be okay."

She nodded, closed her eyes, and tears shot down her cheeks. She was a beautiful woman, and he couldn't stand to see her tormented like this.

"Same plan for him in the Pilot," said the man in the cap. Then he nodded at Doris. "She's got to disappear."

With that Doris broke into tears, sobbing, and saying no, and please, and promising she wouldn't say anything if they just let her go.

The room tilted. Darren felt dizzy and wondered if he might have a concussion. The back of his head had to be scraped badly from hitting the pavement, but he couldn't feel it because his hands were still cuffed in front of him. Blood trickled down his back like a dripping faucet.

"Each of them is going to take both of us," said the bearded guy. "Agreed?"

Beige cap nodded. "I say we do him first. Get it over with." He pointed at Doris. "She can stay in the back bedroom till we get back. That'll buy us a little time to make proper arrangements."

Bearded guy whipped his phone out. "What's the name of the road at the lake?" He must've been looking at his GPS.

"I gave it to you before we left the first time."

"Just tell it to me again!"

"Lanier Ferry something, where it gets all curvy, water on both sides. It's a dam. Buford Dam."

Bearded guy searched his phone. "Got it."

"How long to get there?"

"Seventeen minutes. You still got the needle, right?"

The guy with the cap patted the pocket of his windbreaker. "Affirmative."

It was all so dreamlike that Darren had begun to feel numb to the danger of it all. It was as if he was just going along with it, thinking, "God, it's your responsibility to get me out of this. There's not much more I can do."

Poor Doris didn't deserve to die.

And to think, Pastor Neil Gentry was behind it all.

It was so unreal, Darren thought there must be another explanation, someone else behind all this.

"Get up, lady," said the bearded guy.

Doris looked at Darren with the saddest, weakest, most pitiful eyes he'd ever seen, flooded with tears.

"It's okay," Darren whispered to her.

"Come on." the bearded one said.

"Guys," Darren said, "please don't hurt her. She's no harm to anyone."

"Up!" the bearded man yelled. He pointed at Darren. "Keep your mouth shut."

They really were coming unglued.

Doris cried as she struggled to get to her feet with her hands tied in front of her. The bearded man grabbed her arm, and she squealed as he jerked her to her feet and marched her to the back bedroom.

The man in the cap told Darren to get up. He did so.

The man stared at the couch where Darren had been sitting, then looked at Darren. "Let me see your head."

Darren turned his back to the guy so he could see his head and when he did he noticed the huge bloodstain on the couch where he'd been sitting.

The man looked at his head and cussed. "We need to get you to the car before you pass out or something."

Darren swayed slightly.

The bearded man came back out, saying he'd zip-tied Doris to the headboard.

## CELEBRITY PASTOR

"Let's go," said the guy in the cap. "This guy's bleeding out. Look at the couch."

The bearded man looked over at it and cursed.

"Let's ride."

## THIRTY-FOUR

When Devina stepped into the massive, gleaming penthouse suite at Mission Valley Resort she stopped, dropped her shoulder bag, and slowly turned around, taking in the opulence. Although Morris was blabbing on about where everything was and the bellboy was rolling her suitcase to the master bedroom, Devina could only think that she had never seen a "room" like this before, and probably never would again. Especially after what she was about to do.

"Miss?"

Morris was addressing her.

"Yes, I'm sorry," she said.

"Your massage is in fifteen minutes. Simply take the elevator back down to the main lobby and turn left when you get off. Then follow the signs for the spa. They'll be expecting you."

"Very good." She was ready to get rid of them.

"Champagne is open and on ice at the wet bar along with some goodies." Morris gave a formal wave toward the sleek, gray marble-top bar, which featured the chilled champagne in a shiny black bucket and a spread of crackers, nuts, olives, and cheese.

Morris presented her with a small card. "This is my direct line. Pastor Gentry insists that you have it should you need anything at all. Simply ring me."

With all of the sheer luxury and special attention, Devina felt a ping of regret as she showed them to the door.

She walked over to the floor-to-ceiling windows and looked down at the massive pool area, complete with waterfalls, hot tubs, fire pits, and a tiki bar. Clean-cut teenagers wearing matching khaki shorts, light blue polos, and white tennis shoes hustled back and forth with drink trays and smiles. Tanned and buffed ladies and gentlemen sprawled out on cushy chaise lounges, talking, reading, laughing, and sipping frozen daiquiris.

*All the beautiful people.*

Devina shook it off.

There was no time to dally.

She was regretting her relationship with Saul Dagon and was especially regretting ever getting on the jet to bring her to MVR. She was ready to be home and to be herself again, even if it would mean starting over.

She intended to follow along with Saul's plans—the massage, the Indian dinner, anything he wanted. She would do whatever he said with the sole purpose of making it back home. Then it would all be over, because the world would then know Pastor Neil Gentry had a mistress.

Devina grabbed her overnight bag and found the nearest telephone, situated on a desk near the windows. She sat down, dug around in her bag, and found the phone number she'd scribbled down for Horace Stone, reporter for *The Washington Post*. She followed the instructions on the phone for making a long-distance call and dialed Stone's number, which she assumed was in D.C.

The phone rang three times.

"Come on . . . answer," Devina whispered, her heart racing.

"Horace Stone," came a deep voice.

Devina froze.

She debated changing her mind, hanging up.

"Hello," the man said, questioningly.

"Yes, hello." Her voice sounded quiet and frightened. "I'm the one who emailed you—about Pastor Gentry."

"Yes, yes. I can't tell you how thrilled I was to hear from you. What's your name?"

"I can't tell you that."

There was a brief silence. "Okay . . . you mentioned some damning information."

"Yes," Devina cleared her throat. "I need to be anonymous."

Stone sighed as if to question the legitimacy of the call.

"Do you want to hear what I have to say, or not?" she said.

"Yes, of course. It's just, having a real name to attribute the information to, that just makes it a whole lot more legit."

"Yeah, well if my name comes out, my life will be ruined. So . . ."

"Okay, I get you. But we are all on the record, correct?"

"What do you mean?"

"I mean, everything you tell me, I can use in my story, as long as you're anonymous."

She had a gut check. But then she thought about all Darren McQue had told her about the hurt Saul had caused them—and other women. She thought of the run-in at the restaurant with Don Crane; of Badger showing up at her condo, taking her, and having the place "scrubbed," as if they were mafia; of Saul's sketchy phone call on the Gulfstream about some offer gone bad.

Devina felt used—and no woman ever wanted to feel that.

"Are you there?" Stone said.

"Yes."

"So, are we on the record?"

"Okay. Yes."

"Good. Start wherever you want," he said.

Devina took a deep breath and exhaled. She would be careful not to give any details that would give away her identity.

"The whole time I knew him he went by the name of Saul Dagon. He said he was an oil man from Dallas, Texas, and implied he was single . . ."

FIFTEEN MINUTES TALKING with Horace Stone passed in a flash and Devina did not want to raise any eyebrows by being too late for the massage. She told Stone they would need to talk more within the next day or two and ended the call. She had planned to change, but decided to head straight down to the spa in what she was wearing so she wouldn't be late. She quickly scarfed down a few crackers and cheese and nuts, grabbed her bag, and headed for the door.

She took the elevator to the main floor, exited, and turned left as Morris had instructed. That put her in the lavish lobby where she stood momentarily looking around for signs to the spa, but she saw none.

Feeling an urgency to get where she was supposed to be, she approached the front desk in the lobby. A woman dressed in casual black sportswear appeared to be checking in. A fiftyish brunette with beautiful skin and a gold badge that read 'Lyndsey' was taking care of the woman at the counter.

Devina spoke over them. "Excuse me. Which way to the spa, please?"

The woman checking in turned to face her.

Their eyes met and both women's mouths dropped open.

Devina felt her eyes bulge as she stared at Becky Gentry, whom she recognized instantly from the feature stories she'd read about Pastor Neil Gentry the night before.

The way Becky was staring at Devina made Devina wonder if Becky somehow recognized her — but how could that be?

The brunette employee named Lyndsey had politely pointed in the direction of the spa, but Devina couldn't move.

And Becky Gentry couldn't stop staring at her.

## THIRTY-FIVE

THE SECOND BECKY GENTRY laid eyes on the beautiful young black woman wearing the straw hat and strappy sandals asking for directions to the spa, she knew it was Neil's mistress—the one Darren saw him with at The Oyster the night before.

She just knew it in her heart.

And the young woman recognized Becky, as well. It was obvious because they couldn't take their eyes off one another.

"Mrs. Gentry," the brunette employee got Becky's attention. "I have your key and wi-fi code. Your bags are on their way up to your room, which is one floor below Pastor Gentry, as you requested. And I've jotted his room number on the back of this, also as requested."

Becky took the room key and spoke quietly. "I appreciate it, Lyndsey, and remember, he doesn't know I'm here, so please don't tell anyone. It's a surprise."

Lyndsey beamed, shook her head, and bounced on her toes. "It is completely between us, Mrs. Gentry. We're always so glad to see you. Let me know of anything you should need."

Becky stood there a moment longer, pretending she was getting organized, and decided she would confront the young black woman when she turned around. She would do it quietly. She would insist they go someplace to talk.

Becky took a deep breath, turned around—and the woman was gone.

Becky's pulse pounded and her head spun with rage.

So, Neil had flown this woman—this girl—out here for a fling right after Becky had confronted him about it! *The gall of him.*

Were they sharing a room?

*No way would he be so stupid to take that chance.*

Her blood boiled.

She really did not know the man to whom she was married, and it made her stomach twist in horror.

Becky looked around the busy lobby, making sure Neil was nowhere in sight. She knew if she was ever going to find Neil's mistress again the time was now because she was headed for the spa. But she needed to keep a low profile, because virtually everyone there would recognize her.

Becky threw her carry-on bag over her shoulder and headed in the direction of the spa, getting angrier with every step.

At the end of the long hall, she opened the glass door—etched with the MVR logo—and entered the small, chic lobby. Soft, mystic string music played and candles burned all around, smelling of a mix between vanilla and cinnamon. The walls were made of cork and wood, making it extremely cozy and quiet.

Becky recognized the girl seated behind the small window.

"Hey Krystal," said Becky.

"Mrs. Gentry, what a nice surprise!"

Becky held an index finger to her lips. "Shh. It really is a surprise. Please don't tell anyone I'm here. I'm just going back for a minute. A pretty black girl came in a few minutes ago. Where was she headed?"

Krystal leaned closer to her computer monitor. "She's with Astrid in Valley."

Becky smiled, nodded, and walked to another etched-glass door.

Krystal buzzed it open for her.

Becky walked down the quiet, low-lit hallway, passing the other massage rooms—Horizon, Mountain, Lake, Woods—and arrived at Valley. She took a deep breath, knocked, and went in.

The black woman, who was face down on the massage table and covered in a white sheet, did not look up.

The masseuse, Astrid, looked up instantly and said with surprise, "Mrs. Gentry!"

Then the girl on the table jerked up as if she'd just heard a fire alarm.

"Astrid, good to see you," Becky said, eying the young lady on the table. "Excuse me, please, but I need five minutes with this young lady. If you'll take a quick break . . . and please don't tell anyone I'm here."

"Certainly." Astrid nodded, grabbed a towel for her hands, and slipped out of the room.

The black woman sat up on the edge of the cushioned table and pulled the sheets all around her. Then she stood and slipped her feet into the gold house slippers.

As the door closed, Becky turned to face her. She eyed her up and down. The girl had to be twenty-five and was lean as a rail and built like a Dallas Cowboy cheerleader. Neil could be her father.

"Do you know who I am?" Becky said, crossing her arms.

Devina nodded. "I do."

"You were with my husband at The Oyster last night. What's your name?"

"Devina. I was. But it's about to be over between us."

"Oh, because you've been found out?"

"No. Your husband used me. And I think he's dangerous."

*Dangerous.* That sent a chill down Becky's spine.

"Do you live in Atlanta?" Becky said.

Devina nodded. "I'm from Stone Mountain. But . . . your husband has been providing me with a condo in Midtown."

Becky's heart bulged in her throat and she felt nauseous.

"But you have to know that I thought he was single," Devina said. "He used a fake name with me, Saul Dagon. He said he lived in Dallas and was in the oil business. I didn't know any of this until last night. I didn't know who he was."

Becky could hear and understand the words, but they sounded muffled compared to the roar in her head.

"I'm ending it now. In fact, you should know, I've contacted a reporter with *The Washington Post*. It's going to come out."

Becky teetered.

She shot a hand to the massage table to steady herself.

Devina took a step toward her as if to help.

"Saul—Neil—sent someone to my condo this morning and forced me to come here," Devina said.

Becky made a sound like a crazy laugh and threw her hands up. "Oh, right, I can see you're under duress."

"He arranged this massage, then dinner. I'm going along with it until I can just get home."

"What time is the dinner? Where? What are the plans?"

"I don't know yet. He wants to get Indian food someplace."

Becky knew the restaurant. Neil's favorite Indian food. She could show up there, but the fight they were going to have couldn't be fought in public.

"He stays over with you at this condo in Atlanta?" Becky said.

Devina nodded slowly.

So, those were the nights he was supposed to be in Austin or LA or New York City or wherever.

Becky was dizzy. She fought back tears, not wanting this girl to see her emotions.

Devina was talking—saying she knows sharing a place with Neil was wrong, but she would not have done it if she'd known he was married and had a family.

Every word was like the stab of a knife.

Hunched over now, breathing hard, tears spilling over, Becky found a chair in the corner and sat with a huff.

Devina found a box of tissues and took it to her.

Becky clutched the box in her lap, ripped several out, and wiped her eyes and nose.

"I want you to know how utterly sorry I am," Devina said.

Becky glanced up at her and shook her head.

It wasn't this girl's fault. Neil was the married man. The father. The pastor, for God's sake!

"I just want to go home and get my old life back," Devina said softly.

Becky nodded as if in a trance. "I guess you can do that when you're the mistress."

She thought of the story coming out in *The Washington Post*, of Eli and Hazel finding out, as well as all of their friends and family—and millions of followers.

Their family would be shamed.

Their church would be wounded if not destroyed.

Worst of all, it would be a crushing and insulting blow to the God whom they were supposed to be serving.

Becky blew her nose, dried her eyes, and took an enormous breath as she set her shoulders back and stood.

Dark times were indeed coming. And they would begin right now as the gloves came off with her beloved husband.

# THIRTY-SIX

Pastor Neil Gentry was in his penthouse suite, propped up on the master bed atop its fluffy white down comforter, shoes off, with a glass of Scotch and a bowl of macadamia nuts by his side, browsing through the hundreds of emails on his laptop. Anymore, he only responded to the most pressing emails; dozens upon dozens went without any reply.

He didn't have time.

*Certainly, they understand that.*

The sound of a text pinged on his phone. He reached for it, laid his head back on the pillows, and looked at the screen. It was from Badger:

> I've checked into my room at MVR, sir.

Ah, yes, Neil had heard the door close in the adjoining room several minutes earlier. He'd told Morris to put Badger in the room next to his.

Badger was lucky to still be with him after the blunder his team made back in Atlanta—letting Darren McQue run.

*Idiot.*

Neil texted him back:

> Good. Stand by. Don't leave your room. Get room service if needed.

He tossed the phone back down beside him, set the laptop aside, leaned back, interlocked his fingers behind his head, and closed his eyes.

He told himself this little ordeal would all be behind him soon.

He tried not to think about the fate of Darren McQue, but he couldn't stop himself. He wondered if, well, if he was dead yet. Where they had done it. How? He wondered if Nicole and the kids knew yet.

And what about the old woman? Where would they make her disappear? Who did she leave behind? Would they drop her to the bottom of Lake Lanier with concrete weights?

A pain gripped his chest like a giant metal vice.

"Ohh."

He slowly moved his arms to rest at his side, then laid there very still. It hurt to move.

The same thing had happened several weeks ago in the café at the church, but it had passed quickly.

He took some deep breaths.

He closed his eyes and realized his face was contorted with stress. He tried to relax, but he just couldn't.

He promised once they got through this black cloud, he would be better.

A better person. Like he was before.

No more Badger.

He needed to sleep.

With his eyes closed he decided to recite the twenty-third Psalm as he drifted off . . . but, as much as he tried, he couldn't remember the words.

HE WAS startled awake by the sound of his ringing phone. He got his bearings. He'd fallen asleep. He looked over at the clock on the nightstand and realized he wasn't hurting anymore. *Thank God.* Twenty-five minutes he'd snoozed. He felt for his phone, grabbed it, and looked at the screen, thinking it might be Becky.

Spencer Devereux.

*Ugh.*

Whenever Spencer called there was a fire to put out.

"Yo, go," Neil answered.

"Pastor Neil, we have a problem."

Neil sat up on the edge of the bed, relieved the pain had passed.

"You're always so dramatic. What is it this time?"

He took a sip of his drink, but the glass was sweaty, and the ice cubes had melted. The Scotch was diluted.

"I just played audio from Devina's room at MVR," Spencer said.

A pain shot through Neil's lower back, but it was gone as quick as it had come.

"And?" Neil said impatiently.

"She called Horace Stone. You remember that name?"

Neil's stomach turned and he instantly began to sweat.

"Of course I do. What'd she tell him?"

"She kept herself anonymous, but . . . she unloaded on you. Told about the Atlanta condo, the clothes, the dinners, all expenses paid. And that you stayed over."

Neil was sweating so profusely he staggered to the bathroom, snatched a towel, and wiped his whole head with it.

"Also, and this is the most damaging in my opinion," Devereux said, "she said you went by the name of Saul Dagon and pretended to be a wealthy oil magnate from Dallas. She claimed you even had a LinkedIn page under that name at one time."

Neil bit the towel as hard as he could and saw stars. He cursed into it.

"I know that can't be true, Pastor. Tell me she made that up, that she's lying."

Devereux would find out the truth. There was no use lying to him.

Neil's silence answered his question.

"Oh my gosh," Devereux said. "This is . . . I don't know if we can weather this. I better come out there. Work out damage control."

"Yes. Hurry, will you?"

## THIRTY-SEVEN

Nicole was purposefully taking her good old time in the laundry room while Darren's mom, Sheila, got organized in the guest room. Dottie and Dixie would be dropped off from school any minute and that would help relieve the awkwardness and tension somewhat.

When Sheila had arrived a few minutes earlier, she was particularly cold toward Nicole. After all, Nicole was being portrayed by Pastor Neil Gentry and his church as the aggressor in the sordid affair. That was already a big strike one against Nicole in Sheila's eyes. And now her son Darren was missing, and that was basically strikes two and three put together.

Nicole had explained to her mother-in-law that there was no new word from police about Darren's whereabouts. Sheila had basically turned her back on Nicole and shuffled off to the bedroom where she always stayed when she visited them.

Nicole found herself standing there daydreaming about Darren. About when they'd first met. About their wedding. About how great he had been when the girls were born. About how involved he had been in their lives, their school, their sports, their extracurricular activities.

Sheila sneezed loudly from the guest room upstairs, then again. She'd showed up with a nasty cold and had the awful habit of using the same tissue over and over again.

Nicole had rounded up the kids' dirty clothes and was washing her own as well. As she filled the washer and emptied and folded the clothes from the dryer, she played the moment over and over again in her mind when Becky had sent her the photo of the necklace Neil had given her.

*How did she get her hands on that necklace?*
*Does Neil know she has it?*
*Why did she send it to me all of a sudden?*

Nicole couldn't believe it. Maybe her harsh words had made a difference. Maybe Becky was finally facing what was going on in her husband's secret world. Nicole hoped so with all her heart.

She rested her hands on the warm, churning dryer, and closed her eyes. She whispered, "God, please protect Darren right now, wherever he is. Let him be okay. Bring him home to the girls."

She stopped.

She considered praying for their marriage, but she knew there wasn't much hope for it.

"Be with Becky and Eli and Hazel," she continued. "Protect them from the wrath that's coming to Neil Gentry."

Her phone buzzed in the back pocket of her jeans, and her heart jumped.

She got it out, hands shaking.

*Oh my gosh*, it was Detective Scottie Benson.

"Hello . . ." she answered with bated breath.

"He's alive, Nicole. Darren's alive."

Nicole fell to her knees.

"He's on his way to Northside Hospital. We think he was drugged. His Honda Pilot was run off a steep incline at Buford Dam. They didn't buckle his seat belt and that probably saved his life, because he was ejected from the car. The car actually submerged in the water."

Nicole's shoulders lurched as she cried her eyes out.

"Will he be okay?" her voice cracked.

"We think so. He's got broken bones and a lot of cuts and bruises, but the paramedics were hopeful."

"Thank God," Nicole said. "Thank God."

"The amazing thing was, we got a call from the owner of an Airbnb in Virginia Highlands. He got a call from a neighbor who said something weird was going on at the house. He saw three suspicious looking men in the driveway, one he thought was in handcuffs. The owner called Atlanta PD and they went out and found an elderly woman handcuffed to a bed in the house. She apparently overheard Darren's abductors talking about Buford Dam, so we went out. Found Darren just minutes after the crash."

Nicole was on her feet, scrambling to get her keys. She would have Sheila watch for the girls' arrival home.

She was going to Darren, come hell or high water.

# THIRTY-EIGHT

BEING CONFRONTED in person by Becky Gentry in the spa at MVR was a shock and a wake-up call for Devina Jo Hawkins. In Devina's mind, it was the confirmation she needed to get out of there, to get out of their lives, and never look back.

Once back at her penthouse suite, Devina repacked her suitcase, which didn't require much effort because she had barely unpacked anything. Her plan was to say nothing to anyone at the resort about leaving. All she wanted to do was get back to the airport. When she got there she would find and book the next flight to Atlanta.

She had everything together in no time and was ready to go.

She stopped and looked around the plush suite one last time. She noticed the uncorked champagne that was chilling, so she went over and poured a small amount in one of the flutes. She sipped it and looked at all the fine furnishings.

There would be no more of this luxury and opulence in her foreseeable future. The condo in Atlanta was gone, as was all of the furniture, clothes, jewelry, shoes, and accessories Saul had arranged for her.

It was strange because even though she was nervous about *The Washington Post* story that would be coming out and fearful that her name would be dragged through the mud, she was feeling an energy and excitement she hadn't felt in a long time. She would go home to her roots in Stone Mountain. She would recover at her mom and dad's house where she was always loved unconditionally. Maybe she would see some old friends. And then she would start over again. Cleaner. More optimistic than ever before.

She took her glass and crossed to the hotel phone. Getting a ride wouldn't be quite as easy without her phone. She dialed the front desk. Yes, they did offer a shuttle service to Las Vegas McCarran International Airport every hour, on the hour; it cost eighty dollars. That would go on the room.

*Thanks, Saul.*

She looked at the clock. She'd better get down there, it would be leaving soon.

She stood, threw back the last swallow of Saul's champagne, grabbed her things, and headed for the door.

*Good riddance.*

## THIRTY-NINE

By the time Becky Gentry got to the door of her husband's penthouse suite at MVR, there was no fearful standing around, no rehearsing what she was going to say, no building up courage. It was all there, pent up inside her like a high-pressure hydrogen tank ready to explode. She pounded hard four times and tried the door handle, but it was locked.

She waited in the dark hallway, her heart seemingly ticking audibly like the second-hand of a huge clock.

*Maybe he'll think it's Devina.*

The door opened and Neil stood there holding it, his face morphing from fatigued and bored to high alert panic mode.

Becky barged past him and told him to shut the door.

"Baby, what on earth are you doing here?" he said in a high-pitched tone. "What a nice surprise."

Becky threw her shoulder bag onto the bed, turned to face him, and crossed her arms. "First of all, before you lie to me, I met your other wife Devina at the spa downstairs. Sweet girl."

Neil swallowed so hard it appeared he'd eaten a golf ball.

"You could be her father. Oh, well that's what you are anyway, right? Her sugar daddy?"

"Becky—"

"Don't!" She charged him and shoved him as hard as she

could. "Don't Becky me, you lying, two-faced . . ." She shoved him again, harder.

He fell back several steps and banged into a chair but kept his balance.

"Do you know what you've done?" Becky said. "You've ruined your children's lives. You've ruined *my* life. You've destroyed the church God gave you."

Neil shook his head and ran a hand through his hair. "Honey, let's sit down and talk about this quietly. Please. There's no need to yell."

"That's all you have to say right now, 'There's no need to yell'?" She cranked back and slapped his face as hard as she could. It was loud and stung the flat of her hand. His head swiveled to one side, and he kept it there, as if debating what to do next. She didn't know if he was going to cry or lash out at her.

Becky reached in her pocket and pulled out the necklace he'd given to Nicole as a Christmas present. She fired it at him as hard as she could. It smacked his mouth and dropped to the floor. He stared down at it and touched his lip where the pendant had hit him, then, where she had struck him.

"What's that?" she yelled. "Huh?"

He slowly looked up at her with dead eyes. His upper lip was starting to bleed.

"Look at it, Neil! Look at it!" she yelled. "What is that? Funny, no one knew where that went."

Neil lifted a hand and put an index finger to his lips as if to tell her to lower her voice.

"Don't you tell me to be quiet, you scumbag. How dare you get in front of those people every week. You can't even keep yourself in order. You're *disgusting*. What was the name you used? Saul Dagon? Dallas oil man? You're *sick*, Neil."

He took several steps toward her, both hands up, as if trying to tame a wild animal.

She backed up and clenched her teeth so hard she saw stars. He continued toward her.

"Don't come near me! You filthy—"

"If you will stop yelling, perhaps I can explain some things."

"You want to explain some things? Explain why you made fun of me to Nicole McQue. Huh? Why you two laughed together about my out-of-control spending. Explain why you had intimate talks with her about me wanting to be in the limelight and about me being so in love with clothes and houses that I wouldn't care if you had an affair!"

His face had turned crimson, and his mouth was locked open as if he'd just seen a pack of zombies. A drop of blood hung from his upper lip. The cheek she had slapped was bright red.

"You've ruined our marriage, Neil. Not me. It wasn't me. I have my faults, but I'm not the one who couldn't keep my pants on."

Becky put her hands on her waist and dropped her head, out of breath, totally spent, wanting it to be over. Then she looked up at him. "You're sick, Neil. Seriously. You need help."

"Becky, we can get through this. Please. Devereux is on his way. He'll know what to do. We can say—"

"Listen to yourself!" she yelled. "You want to keep lying your way along while your heart is *sick*. Don't you have any remorse? What's happened to you, Neil? You have truly lost your way."

"Oh, come on, Becky. It's not like you haven't enjoyed the ride. You've loved every minute of it. You have—"

"Until now! Now I hate every minute of it, and I hate you. Your playmate told me she's contacted *The Washington Post*. It's all going to come down on you."

"And you," he said. "It's coming down on you, too."

*What an impudent child.*

Becky huffed and shook her head. "You really are sick. You're demented. You don't care about me, or your children. All you care about is *yourself*. You're a narcissist. And a control freak. I'm done."

There was a knock at the door.

Neil walked toward it, apparently welcoming the reprieve.

"Don't you get that," Becky ordered. "We're not finished here."

Neil mumbled something and kept going. He opened the door slightly.

"I heard a commotion," said a deep male voice. "Is everything alright?"

"My wife's here," Neil whispered. "Just a family squabble."

Becky wasn't having it. She crossed quickly to the door and opened it wide. "Who are you?"

A dark-haired man with a scruffy, sparse dark beard looked at Neil.

"Don't look at him," Becky said. "Answer me. Who are you?"

Neil turned to her and took hold of one of her wrists and tried desperately to keep things calm by speaking in a quiet, even tone. "He's part of the team. He's with me, with us. Remember, we talked about security? That's all it is."

Becky eyed the man a second longer and ripped her wrist out of Neil's grasp.

The man's dark presence . . . something was terribly wrong.

For a half-second, she wondered if she might be in danger.

"This whole thing has gotten so messed up." She turned her back on them and walked back into the room. She crossed to the huge windows and looked out over the massive pool area, sizing up her next move.

She heard the door latch closed behind her.

She continued looking out at the pool and said, "It was true about Brenda Vincent, wasn't it. I knew. Deep down, I knew. And what about Darren? Nicole said he didn't come home last night."

Becky turned around to continue and stopped cold. Ice cold.

The man was in the room.

He was standing next to Neil with his fingers locked in front of him like a humble waiter.

"What's he doing in here?" Becky said, with a sudden chill.

Neil walked over to the wet bar. The man remained where he was, near the door. "I told you, he's security," Neil said as he poured two fingers of Scotch into a clean glass.

Becky's stomach felt sick.

She was scared.

The man was dark and seedy looking. Becky sensed danger. Real danger.

How had Neil bent to such lows?

A phone buzzed across the room. It was the man's phone. He got it out of his pocket and glanced at the screen. "I need to take this, sir. I'll be right back. Excuse me." He left the room with his ear to the phone as he went.

"What is going on, Neil? Why is he here?" Becky said. "This is between us."

Neil took a neat sip from his glass and looked at her. He simply shook his head. He walked over to where the necklace was still on the floor, bent over, picked it up, and dropped it in his pocket.

"It's over," Becky said. "You're ruined. Between me and Nicole and *The Washington Post*—it's finished." She began to walk straight for the door, feeling a ping of apprehension. "I'm going home. I'll be leaving you."

Neil set his drink down gently, then darted toward the door, cutting her off there. "Don't go yet," he said in a huff. "At least wait till Spencer gets here. Listen to his plan."

Becky's head craned back, and she squinted at him as if he was from another planet.

A quick knock at the door.

Neil opened it.

"I need to speak with you," the man said in a serious tone.

Neil pushed the door open. "Come in and talk. No more secrets."

The man caught the door with one hand and stared at Neil, questioningly.

Neil nodded for him to come in.

Becky felt a terrible sense of foreboding.

The man stepped inside and let the door close behind him.

"The, ah . . . the accident did not go as planned," the man said quietly.

Neil suddenly wound up and threw his glass. It shattered against a far wall.

Becky screamed.

*Darren! He's talking about Darren.*

Her hands were flat against her chest in horror.

"He was thrown from the car. He's in the hospital. He's going to live."

Neil grunted as if shocked with a taser.

"Police found the old lady. She's talking, too."

Neil's hands shot to his chest. His eyes bulged twice their size. The veins and bones in his neck protruded grossly.

Becky had never seen Neil look like this. Something was wrong, physically. But she could do nothing. She could not move. She was in shock. Everything had flicked to slow motion.

"Sir?" The bad man stepped toward Neil, reached a hand out as if to steady him, but then pulled away with an illuminated expression of fright etched on his face.

Neil dropped to the floor like a concrete statue that had been shoved over.

He hit the ground with such utter force and such a dreadful thud, Becky knew he was already dead.

# FORTY

Nicole had sat in a chair next to Darren's hospital bed in post-op for hours waiting for him to wake up from surgery. Sheila had been home when Dottie and Dixie got dropped off from school that afternoon and was staying overnight with them, as planned.

It was after midnight when Darren finally opened his eyes.

He blinked and squinted from the bright lights.

Then his pretty green eyes found Nicole, now standing by his bed, leaning over him, a hand covering one of his hands, which was bruised and plugged with tubes and wrapped in places with white tape.

His head was bandaged with gauze and several spots of blood had penetrated through. One arm was wrapped the same way, also with blood spots showing through. His right leg was in a cast.

Darren looked from Nicole down to his injured limbs, only moving his eyes.

"You're going to be okay," Nicole whispered. "You're pretty banged up, but the doctors say you should make a full recovery."

"The girls?" he whispered.

She nodded. "They're just fine. Your mom is staying with them at the house tonight. She said to tell you she loved you and she'll see you soon."

He sighed and nodded.

"There was an older woman with me . . ." he said with a dry voice.

"She's fine. She wasn't hurt. And her dog was waiting for her on the front porch of her house when she got home."

"How . . ."

Nicole pulled the chair close, sat down, and explained how the police got involved and eventually found him.

He could only sigh and blink. A lone tear rolled out one eye to the pillow.

"Can you handle more big news?" Nicole said.

He nodded.

"Are you sure? This is mind-blowing."

He nodded again.

"Neil Gentry died today."

His eyes flicked to meet hers.

"He had a massive heart attack at the resort in Las Vegas. Becky had flown out there today and confronted him — about everything."

Darren let out a huge sigh, shook his head, and closed his eyes.

"Becky called me a couple hours ago to check on you," Nicole said softly. "She apologized about everything. She found the necklace he gave me."

"Wow," Darren said.

"I know."

They sat in silence for a long time with her hand covering his.

She broke the quiet first with a whisper. "I know you may not want to hear this, but I love you. I want to be your wife and the mother of our girls for as long as we live."

Darren's head turned slightly toward her, and he locked eyes with hers.

"I'm so sorry about what happened," she whispered. "I hope you'll forgive me. I can't take it back, but I can promise to love you and only you from this day forward. That I can do, and I promise I will . . ."

He turned over the hand she had been covering and squeezed her hand as best he could.

With that slight gesture, Nicole started to cry.

And so did he.

A spirit of hope and promise seemed to rise between them.

She got tissues from her purse, stood, leaned over him, and wiped his eyes, then her own.

"Will you bring me something from home?" he whispered. "Top left dresser drawer."

She sniffed, and smiled, and nodded, and felt her heart soar because she knew what he was about to say.

*"My wedding ring."*

# EPILOGUE

*The Washington Post* – 6 Months later

**A Celebrity Pastor: His Crimes, His Death, and the Aftermath for His Church & Followers**

By Horace Stone

The sins and the death of celebrity pastor Neil Gentry last August rocked the religious world then and are still impacting lives and sending out shockwaves today.

Gentry's former church, Vine & Branches, used to be one of the fastest growing in the world, with campuses in Atlanta, LA, Austin, NYC, and a TV ministry spanning the globe.

Since Gentry's sudden death of a massive heart attack last August in Las Vegas, however, Gentry's crimes, his toxic controlling and manipulative leadership, and his sexual misconduct have sent his former church and many of its leaders and congregants into an ugly tailspin.

Immediately following Gentry's death at his prized Mission Valley Resort, the church went into crisis mode and hired Interim Pastor Bailey Bridges of Los Angeles in an attempt to right the ship. But over the months to come Vine & Branches could not pull out of its nosedive. All TV and media contracts with Vine &

# EPILOGUE

Branches—totaling tens of millions of dollars—were canceled. And all of the churches within the Vine & Branches umbrella left the network to become their own independent religious entities. All changed their names and mission statements. None are thriving. Many have closed their doors for good.

For several months after Gentry's death, the deacons and leaders of Vine & Branches Church denied any wrongdoing and continued serving at the church. It was only recently, months after Gentry was posthumously found guilty in two cases of attempted murder and multiple cases of sexual harassment, that most of the elders and top leaders apologized to victims. All of the leaders under Gentry eventually resigned their positions and left the church. Gentry's executive assistant, Spencer Devereux, and three other men from outside the church, have been charged with two counts of attempted murder, and are awaiting trial in Atlanta.

In speaking at length with many of those former elders, leaders, and long-time volunteers, many are suffering profoundly from traumatic aftereffects of their time under Gentry's leadership at Vine & Branches. None wanted to speak on record, but most did agree to share anonymously and did so often with quiet, simmering rage and cathartic tears about their lingering struggles with shame, depression, sleeplessness, guilt, addiction, and even financial hardship. Sadly, 68 percent of those interviewed have left organized religion altogether.

Dr. Asher Jenkins, a Christian psychologist from Wheaton, Illinois, sympathized with those suffering in the aftermath of the Vine & Branches implosion, and attempted to offer hope.

"It is not about your church or your brand of church, or your group, or how big you are, or your pastor, or what you offer," Jenkins said. "It is about loving Jesus and loving people. That is the one true safeguard. Jesus himself said we could simplify all his commands by doing two things: love the Lord your God with all your heart, soul, mind, and strength—and love your neighbor as yourself. Do that and remain humble. Be proactive about seeking accountability. Be spiritually prepared *before* the crisis hits."

# DISCUSSION QUESTIONS FOR CELEBRITY PASTOR

1) In the chapter 1 interview between *Washington Post* reporter Horace Stone and Clinical Psychologist and Trauma Expert Dr. Daryl Kit, the following subjects were addressed. Spend a bit of time discussing each:

- Churches with insular cultures
- The immense popularity of the pastor
- Lack of accountability in leadership
- The fallout/damage done to those in a congregation negatively impacted by a leader's demise

2) Nicole McQue explained to Dr. Yeager that she only got to see her daughters occasionally and when she did it hurt badly. She said: "When I do see them, things aren't the same. I can see it in their faces, in their eyes. They're hurting. They don't look healthy, not like they used to. They don't feel the same about me. They know I did something wrong." Discuss the aftereffects of a marital affair, what it does to families and children, and why it must be avoided at all costs.

3) Continue your discussion about question number two by discussing and brainstorming specific things married couples can

DISCUSSION QUESTIONS FOR CELEBRITY PASTOR

do to remain happy, healthy, and truly satisfied in their marital relationships.

4) Early on in the book we learn bits and pieces about Nicole McQue's questionable relationship with Pastor Neil Gentry. Nicole is married to Darren, and they have two girls. Discuss the problems Nicole and Darren will certainly face if they attempt to move forward together, and the possible solutions to those challenges.

5) When the McQue family first started attending Vine & Branches Church they loved serving and volunteering. After time, however, they felt they were being taken advantage of. They were no longer serving God, but man. Have you experienced this? If so, what happened and how was it resolved? What is your mindset about serving and volunteering? When do you say yes? Is it okay to say no?

6) When Nicole McQue meets with Dr. Samuel Yeager, she gets the chance to talk about what's happened in her marriage and church life, and what the future may hold. Do you think it's helpful to confide in someone else about the challenges in your life? Do you have someone you can confide in? Discuss.

7) When Nicole McQue is being interviewed by the church elders and attorney, her husband Darren says: "God knows what's going on. He sees everything. This will not prosper." Do you have that kind of faith in God? Discuss Darren's statement, how it applied to the story, and how it may apply in your lives.

8) Becky Gentry made many excuses for her husband, Pastor Neil Gentry. She kept telling herself that he was an important man, in high demand, under lots of pressure, and that they were no ordinary couple. Why did she do this? What was wrong with her thinking, and what did it lead to?

9) At one point in the story, Becky Gentry reflected on how her husband's sermons used to use truths from the Bible to deliver

poignant messages. But, she was realizing things had changed, he had changed. He had started caring more about his appearance and his approval than about keeping God as the focal point of his sermons. Apparently, Pastor Gentry had lost sight of the scripture in John 17:17 that reads: "Sanctify them in the truth; Your word is truth." Discuss the importance of utilizing scripture in sermons.

10) Nicole McQue tells Dr. Samuel Yeager: "As mad as I am at Neil Gentry, I'm even madder at the church leaders who I loved and respected and served with. They didn't believe me, and they failed to protect me. And now they're trying to throw me under the bus in order to protect their leader." Have you experienced hurt or abuse from the church? Briefly, what happened and how have you attempted to overcome it? Have you been successful?

11) In chapter 26, Darren is offered a bribe to remain silent. If he does not accept the bribe he will be killed. If you were Darren, what would you have done in that situation? Why? Discuss.

12) God continued to grow Vine & Branches Church even when Pastor Neil Gentry and his wife Becky had wandered far from him. Becky thought perhaps it had been a mistake to use the growth of the church as a litmus test to determine how well she/they were doing spiritually. Discuss.

13) At one point, Becky Gentry expressed guilt because God was nowhere on her list of priorities. Do you ever feel this way? Discuss.

14) Late in the story in the office at Mission Valley Resort when speaking to Badger on the phone, Pastor Gentry feels like he's having a panic attack. He thinks, *God is punishing you. He's had enough. You need to confess. Repent. Step down.* Then he envisions the headlines and news reels about the scandalous collapse; the hurt and outrage in Becky's eyes; the murmuring and judgement that would blaze through Vine & Branches like wildfire; the disappointment and possible rebellion in Eli and Hazel; the endless police investigations; the trials and jail time. Discuss this

critical juncture in Pastor Gentry's life. What should he have done? What could have happened? How could things have turned out differently?

15) Discuss your thoughts and feelings on the quote at the end of the book from the Christian psychologist when he says: "It is not about your church or your brand of church, or your group, or how big you are, or your pastor, or what you offer. It is about loving Jesus and loving people. That is the one true safeguard. Jesus himself said we could simplify all his commands by doing two things: love the Lord your God with all your heart, soul, mind, and strength—and love your neighbor as yourself. Do that and remain humble. Be proactive about seeking accountability. Be spiritually prepared *before* the crisis hits."

## WHAT'S NEXT FROM CRESTON?

If you're ready to start Creston's latest series, check out book one in the Signs of Life Series on **Amazon**:

# ABOUT THE AUTHOR

**Creston Mapes** grew up in northeast Ohio, where he has fond memories of living with his family of five in the upstairs portion of his dad's early American furniture store - The Weathervane Shop. Creston was not a good student, but the one natural talent he possessed was writing.

He set type by hand and cranked out his own neighborhood newspaper as a kid, then went on to graduate with a degree in journalism from Bowling Green State University. Creston was a newspaper reporter and photographer in Ohio and Florida, then moved to Atlanta, Georgia, for a job as a creative copywriter.

Creston served for a stint as a creative director, but quickly learned he was not cut out for management. He went out on his own as a freelance writer in 1991 and, over the next 30 years, did work for Chick-fil-A, Coca-Cola, The Weather Channel, Oracle,

## ABOUT THE AUTHOR

ABC-TV, TNT Sports, colleges and universities, ad agencies, and more. He's ghost-written more than ten non-fiction books.

Along the way, Creston has written many contemporary thrillers, achieved Amazon Bestseller status multiple times, and had one of his novels (*Nobody*) optioned as a major motion picture.

Creston married his fourth-grade sweetheart, Patty, and they have four amazing adult children. Creston loves his part-time job as an usher at local venues where he gets to see all the latest-greatest concerts and sporting events. He enjoys reading, fishing, thrifting, bocci, painting, pickleball, time with his family, and dates with his wife.

To keep informed of special deals, giveaways, new releases, and exclusive updates from Creston, sign up for his newsletter at: **CrestonMapes.com/contact**

To view all of Creston's eBooks, audiobooks, and paperbacks go to **Amazon.com/author/crestonmapes**

ABOUT THE AUTHOR

## STAND ALONE THRILLERS
*Celebrity Pastor*
*I Am In Here*
*Nobody*

## SIGNS OF LIFE SERIES
*Signs of Life*
*Let My Daughter Go*
*I Pick You*
*Charm Artist*
*Son & Shield*
*Secrets in Shadows*

## THE CRITTENDON FILES
*Fear Has a Name*
*Poison Town*
*Sky Zone*

## ROCK STAR CHRONICLES
*Dark Star: Confessions of a Rock Idol*
*Full Tilt*